"Part history, part pure fantasy in the tradition of the Arabian Nights, Steve Paulsen's Dream Weaver is the thrilling story of a generous and courageous young man whose dreams have unusual properties. When he sets out to learn the truth of his past, he meets the beautiful and feisty Rose, and together, they journey across a beautifully nuanced landscape."
—**Isobelle Carmody**, best-selling YA author.

"A magical blend of fantasy and history, this book takes the reader on a wondrous adventure through exotic locations and amazing dreamscapes, into the furthest reaches of the imagination. I loved every word!"
—**George Ivanoff**, Multi-award winning kids and YA author of the *You Choose* and *Other Worlds* book series, and the popular non-fiction *Survival Guides* series.

"Steven Paulsen's YA historical fantasy diligently charts a dreamer boy's bare feet sprinting along a vivid Mediterranean backdrop and stumbling across the vast Bādiyat Ash-Shām desert. In a world where the port is a marketplace for crafty begging, dreams summon taste and cartwheel in multihues. Dream Weaver is a fast-paced, seascape and desertscape escapade, vibrant with discernment and a hearty sense of place."
—**Eugen Bacon**, World Fantasy Finalist and award-winning author of *Danged Black Thing, Mage of Fools* and *Chasing Whispers.*

T0244791

Dream Weaver

Steven Paulsen

This is a work of fiction. The events and characters portrayed herein are imaginary and are not intended to refer to specific places, events or living persons. The opinions expressed in this manuscript are solely the opinions of the author and do not necessarily represent the opinions of the publisher.

Dream Weaver

ISBN-13: 978-1-922856-35-7

V1.0

Printed in Palatino Linotype and Aladin Regular

IFWG Publishing Australia

www.ifwgaustralia.com

For Jack and Hannah

and for Sarah, Laura and Edward

with love.

Map of Anatolia and Surrounding Regions, with Notable Landmarks in *Dream Weaver*

Hope is a waking dream.

—Aristotle

Anatolia—Autumn, 1405 AD.

1. Death of a Fisherman

Ali dashed barefoot along the rough-cobbled back alleys of Korykos, threading his way through the city towards the seafront at Fisherman's Cove. He shoved past jostling groups of early morning market-goers, skipped around a tethered goat, and dodged a scrawny, stray dog that yapped and snapped at his heels.

Hasan the fisherman's life was at stake. Ali had to warn him not to take his boat out or he would die. Heart pounding, Ali lurched onto the sandy beach. He gasped in the tangy sea air as he scanned the blue-green water for boats. The Mediterranean Sea stretched empty all the way to the horizon, the vista broken only by the small fortified island known as the Maiden's Castle lying a short distance offshore.

The fishermen were still making ready to head out. Ali spotted Hasan in the shallows, preparing to launch his boat, and let out a huge breath.

"Stop," he called, sprinting across the pale sand and splashing into the cool water. "Don't take your boat out! Tiger sharks will tear you to bits if you do."

Hasan guffawed. "What do you reckon?" he called to half a dozen men mending nets on the beach. "This skinny little urchin reckons sharks'll get me if I take my boat out."

A weaselly, hook-nosed fisherman hawked and spat onto the sand. "Ain't likely, Hasan. But if the kid's right, at least it'll be quicker than drinking yourself to death."

There were a few snorts of laughter and Weasel and the others went back to their work.

"I dreamed about you last night," Ali said, pointing his finger at Hasan. "I saw what will happen."

Hasan scowled and raised a clenched fist. "You'll see *this* in your dreams if you don't shut up."

"You're talking nonsense," said a wiry little fisherman with a scruffy white turban tied around his head. "The sharks leave us alone if we leave them alone." Nevertheless, he fingered the *nazar* bead amulet hanging on a leather thong around his neck to ward off the evil eye.

"If Hasan goes out in his boat today," Ali said, throwing his hands in the air in an *I give up* gesture, "he *will* die."

Hasan cursed and shoved him in the chest. Ali was short for his age, not much over half the brute's height, and the blow sent him staggering back, thin arms cartwheeling. He hit the water with a loud splash and went under. By the time he struggled to his feet, coughing and spluttering, Hasan had already climbed aboard his boat, raised the sail and was guiding his small craft across the shallows.

Ali pushed his long black hair out of his eyes and stood watching, waves lapping at his knees, until Hasan had sailed past the whitewater shoals near the Maiden's Castle, and out into the deeper sapphire-blue water beyond. Then he waded back to the shore, dripping wet and despondent.

He pulled off his faded olive-green vest and wrung the sea water from it. The fabric was threadbare in places, the edges frayed where most of the original white embroidery was now long gone. He shrugged back into it, pulled the tattered scarlet sash tight around his waist to hold up his baggy, raw-cotton *şalvar* trousers, and checked that his dagger and calf-skin purse were secure. Then he turned to look back out to sea.

Hasan was manoeuvring his boat to where the fish would be running, to where Ali *knew* the fisherman would meet his end. He had an overwhelming sense that the strange dream he had had was prophetic, that it would come true.

To anyone else observing the situation, there was no sign of anything amiss. The pale-blue sky was cloudless, and a gentle breeze made the flat aquamarine sea glint here and there with sparkles of autumn sunlight. Flocks of noisy seagulls swooped and wheeled overhead. The men on the beach continued to mend their nets. The stall-holders with their baskets full of calamari, red mullet and silver anchovies bartered with customers, and boat-builders sawed and hammered the timbers of their trade.

Then all of a sudden, the water around Hasan's boat churned and frothed, alive with large, darting shapes, dorsal fins breaking the surface. An enormous blue-green shark with dark stripes across its body surged out of the water. It twisted in the air, its pale-yellow underbelly visible, and crashed back into the sea.

On shore, a woman screamed.

The cry started a commotion. Fishermen, stall-holders and boat-builders alike left their work to come and stare. Shoppers and pedestrians stood gaping, open-mouthed. The growing crowd looked on in disbelief.

"How can this be?" asked an old sailor in the throng. "Never seen tiger sharks in the sea this far east. And never seen them hunt in a pack like this."

But before anyone could answer, Hasan's pinewood boat suddenly reared up and splintered into pieces. There were gasps and screams from the watching people, now numbering fifty or more, as the blood-hungry tiger sharks leaped and thrashed in the now red-frothed water, fighting among themselves for pieces of the ill-fated man's flesh.

"God's mercy be with him," said Weasel.

Someone else remarked on the dead man's misfortune and the oddness of the attack. People muttered to themselves. Voices rose in anger.

Ali pushed clear of the milling crowd and made his wet and miserable way back across the sand towards the Old City. He felt sick in his stomach, full of remorse that he had been unable to stop Hasan.

"That's him," a man shouted. "The skinny kid on the beach."

There were angry cries and Ali realised, too late, that the crowd had turned into a mob.

"We heard him put a curse on poor old Hasan," Weasel said.

"Get him!" another voice yelled.

Ali took off at a run, his heart in his throat, the enraged fishermen in pursuit. He scrabbled up the grassy slope beyond the beach, and turned onto the cobbled esplanade along the seafront. He raced along it, away from the old stone castle towering high on a bluff over the city, and slipped into a gap between a pair of tall timber buildings standing so close together that he had to twist sideways to squeeze between them. He emerged into a network of cobbled lanes, sprinting along one after another in his attempt to get away.

But his flight came to an abrupt halt when he rounded a corner and found the way was blocked by a low, wide ox-cart piled high with bulging sacks of grain. There was no room to pass. It crawled inexorably along the lane towards him, a pair of plodding brown oxen being led by a farmer holding a thick hemp rope tethered to their heavy wooden yoke.

Ali turned to go back, but the sounds of the outraged fishermen were closing in. He cast desperately about for some way out, and realised his only option was a shallow doorway in one of the tall, two-storey buildings flanking the lane. But the cart was almost upon it. He sprang between the farmer and oxen, jumped the tether rope, and flung himself into the doorway, narrowly avoiding the wide, curved horns of the nearest ox.

The cart slid in front of him, sacks of grain grazing his chest and face, hiding him from view. From the sound of the angry voices coming from the top of the lane, his pursuers could not agree which way he had gone.

"Hey you," one of the fishermen called to the ox-cart driver, "did you see a boy run past here?"

But the farmer only told them to get out of the way, and Ali gave a gratified sigh of relief, guessing the man either didn't want to get involved or didn't like fishermen.

When the cart had passed, Ali stepped from the doorway and hurried to the opposite end of the lane where it intersected with a busy street. He paused briefly at the corner, deciding which way to go, and noticed a heavily-built, black-bearded Uzbeg mercenary scrutinising him from the other side of the street.

The soldier looked to be a steppe nomad, probably one of the many who had fought with the barbaric Turko-Mongol conqueror,

Timur Lenk, when he overran and subjugated the Ottoman Empire. But unlike the other nomad mercenaries who had found their way to Korykos looking for easy money in the chaos and unrest since Timur's untimely death and the collapse of his army, this one was armoured with lamellar on his upper arms, leather greaves below his knees and a chainmail shirt over his chest.

While not a fisherman, the Uzbeg was still a potential threat who might remember and report seeing him if there was profit to be gained. Still, there was nothing Ali could do about it, so he turned his back on the mercenary and hurried into the old part of the city. He cut through the Jewish quarter, then past the blue-tiled mosque with its towering minarets, keeping to the back lanes he knew so well, avoiding the busy market square where he might be recognised.

His flight brought him to a lane that came to a dead end at a high wooden fence. He glanced around to make sure he was not being observed, climbed the fence and dropped to the other side. There, he slithered down a grassy bank and set off at a trot along a narrow dirt track that skirted the bank of the Karyağdi River.

After a while the river took a turn and the bank widened, before it twisted back and cut a deep gorge through the land, before emptying into the Mediterranean Sea. Ali slowed to a halt where the grass grew lush, the bank was lined with fragrant myrtle bushes, and a gnarled grandfather olive tree provided shade. It was one of the few peaceful spots in the crumbling Old City, if one could stand the pervasive stink from a nearby drain that emptied into the river.

Ali squatted on his haunches beneath the tree's whispering foliage, the plump green olives dotting its branches almost ready for harvest. He heaved a long sigh of relief at his escape. Not that this was the end of his problems by any means, not while the fishermen believed he had cursed one of them.

He picked up some small stones, and threw them one by one into the river. He was a good shot, better than most of his friends, and usually delighted in target practice. But today he tossed them without much effort, distracted by his thoughts.

Ali knew Hasan's death was not his fault, but he felt guilty because he had known what was going to happen and been unable to stop the fisherman. The dream he'd had about it was like no other, vivid and realistic, but strangely misted with a ruby-red tinge. When he woke from it, it had left him with an unusual coppery taste in his mouth and a strange sense of certainty it would come true. Why had this dream come to him? Why had he been so *certain* it was going to happen?

A couple of nights earlier, Hasan had knocked Ali unconscious in a drunken rage in the taverna where he worked clearing tables and cleaning up. When he came to, Ali had had a bloody nose, a pounding head, and a vengeful wish to see the fisherman pay. Hasan was a drunkard and a bully, but Ali had not wanted him to die.

Brushing away the small, sticky flies that were bothering his face, Ali suddenly caught sight of a pair of fishermen armed with gutting knives on the other side of the river. His eyes bulged in alarm. They had seen him and were signalling to someone on *his* side of the river.

He lurched to his feet and turned to run, but saw a third fisherman, a brawny Armenian with a bald, egg-shaped head advancing on him. Ali spun around the other way, only to find himself confronted by Weasel, the hook-nosed man from the beachfront at Fisherman's Cove, now wielding a long gutting blade that looked more like a short sword than a knife.

There was nowhere to run. Wiping the sweat from his forehead, Ali drew his own small dagger in a white-knuckled grip and took up a defensive fighting stance. As the men converged on him, he swivelled to face first one man then the other, blinking rapidly.

Weasel rushed him, feinting with his wicked blade.

Ali dodged and skipped aside, only to have something that felt like a runaway horse crash into him from behind and knock the breath out of him. He hit the ground hard, a heavy weight on top of him, and everything went dark for a moment.

When Ali regained his senses, he was on his back, dust and blood in his mouth, the egghead straddling him, pinning his thin wrists to the ground with his large, work-calloused hands.

"Got 'im!" the man yelled in triumph.

2. Out of the Frying Pan

Ali thrashed and kicked, but could not dislodge Egghead.

"Be still," Weasel snapped. He strode over and waved the point of his gutting knife in Ali's face.

Ali slumped back and glared at his captors.

"Watch out for his evil eye," Weasel said, making a protective horned-hand gesture.

Both men averted their gaze. They had *nazar* symbols freshly painted on their foreheads, like Buddhist third eyes.

Ali studied the symbol on Egghead's forehead. It had a black pupil surrounded by three concentric rings; the iris or first ring was pale blue, the next ring was white like the white of a human eye, and third was an outline of cobalt blue.

It was hypnotic.

It seemed to look straight into him, and for a moment Ali wondered if he *was* evil, if Hasan's death *was* his fault. Then he snapped free of the thought and turned his attention back to the fishermen.

"Those *nazar* eyes won't help you," Ali jeered, preying on their superstition.

Egghead thrust his face into Ali's, a throbbing vein bulging in his forehead, rage burning in his eyes. "Tengri curse you," he hissed, invoking the old god, still followed by many despite the coming of the Romans, Jews, Christians and Muslims, his rotten-tooth breath nearly making Ali gag.

"Get him up," Weasel said. "Here come the others."

Egghead manhandled Ali to his feet and held him in a crushing bear hug.

Weasel hailed the other pair of fishermen running towards them along the river bank.

It's now or never, Ali thought. He slammed the heel of his foot into Egghead's knee.

The man buckled forward, howling in pain.

Ali drove his head back into Egghead's nose. Bone and gristle gave way with a sickening crunch, blood spurted, and the man let go of his grip with a cry. Ali lurched free, scooped up his dagger from where it had fallen, and whirled around to run.

But Weasel sprang at him, lips drawn back in a snarl, gutting knife raised.

Ali glanced in despair at his own small dagger; then, in a flash of inspiration, he thrust his free hand at Weasel's face, palm forward, fingers spread, in an Armenian black magic curse gesture.

The effect was immediate, all that Ali had hoped for and more. Weasel dropped his knife and fell back, desperately trying to make another horned-hand protection sign. Ali turned and scrambled up the steep river bank, grabbing clumps of weeds and myrtle, using his dagger as a climbing spike to haul himself to the top.

The other two fishermen arrived at a run, puffing and yelling. They lunged after him, but were a moment too late. Ali leaped to his feet at the top of the bank and their knives swished through empty air behind him. He gave them a brief glance as they struggled to clamber up the bank after him, sheathed his dagger and took off along the narrow, cobbled street towards the bazaar.

Ali ran hard to put some distance between himself and his pursuers, but when he approached the old part of the city he slowed to a less conspicuous pace. His plan was to cut through the bazaar to the docks on the other side of the bay, an area the fishermen shunned due to a festering dispute with the dockers and harbour men. He would have to hide out there for some time to come. The fishermen were a close-knit bunch and would not readily forget Hasan's death, nor Ali's supposed role in it.

Ali reached the bazaar district and melted into the throng of market-goers, merchants and travellers. He moved easily among them, but stayed alert, watching and listening for any sign of trouble. The scent of aromatic oils, the dusty odour of warm animal dung, and the fragrance of pungent spices all competed for air space.

He was momentarily disconcerted when a group of Chagatai nomad mercenaries, probably Uzbegs, paused their haggling at an apple stall to watch him hurry past. He wondered fleetingly what their interest was in him, but quickly forgot about them when his stomach growled with hunger pangs. In his haste to warn Hasan about the tiger sharks he had gone without breakfast. Now it was late morning and he was starving.

Ali passed a coppersmith's shop, shiny engraved copper pots, ewers and platters on display, the metallic *tuk-tuk-tuk* of a wooden mallet beating a sheet of copper ringing out from within. He came to a halt beside a woodcarver's workshop, opposite a smoky stall emitting a particularly delicious aroma.

There, beneath a blue-and-white-striped canopy, a fat turbaned man known as "Big-hands" perspired, red-faced, over a hot charcoal grill. The spicy kebabs he made with chunks of swordfish marinated in lemon juice, olive oil and his own secret spice blend were renowned throughout the city. With good reason, as Ali well knew. It made his mouth water thinking about them.

He blinked away the flies and dust, looked left and right, then darted around a stack of clay water jars and across the alley to the kebab stall.

"Big-hands, quick! Six of your famous kebabs."

The man's eyes went wide. "Ali!"

"Hurry," Ali said, glancing over his shoulder. "I've got to get out of here."

Big-hands pulled uncomfortably at the collar of his grey cotton kaftan. "Umm… They're not quite ready," he said.

Ali frowned. "They look done to me."

Big-hands raised his shoulders in an exaggerated shrug. "It's hard to tell with fresh fish."

"*Fresh* fish…" Ali thought.

Their eyes met, and Ali recognised betrayal, guilt written on Big-hands' face. The fishermen had already been here…

Big-hands lunged for him.

Ali side-stepped the attack, snatched a handful of kebab sticks right off the hot grill, and took off at a run along the lane.

"He's here," Big-hands bellowed, giving chase. "Ali is here!"

Ali pushed between the market-goers with practised ease, confident in his ability to elude his pursuer, but when he slowed to dodge a group of small children playing marbles in the dirt, he glanced over his shoulder and did a double-take. Big-hands was bearing down on him, face flushed, eyes bulging, a cleaver clutched in his raised fist.

Then Ali tripped over a sack of red lentils in front of a streetside stall and sprawled on his knees, lentils spilling everywhere.

The stallholder yelled and swore at him.

Big-hands roared in triumph.

Ali jumped to his feet, the purloined kebabs still miraculously in his clutches, ducked aside to avoid Big-hand's cleaver, and took off again, ignoring his scraped knees.

It was too much for Big-hands, now doubled over and gasping. "By God," he said between breaths. "When I get hold of you…I will throttle you…and chop you into little pieces."

Big-hands' strength was legendary. It was said that he'd once crushed a prized coconut brought overland by camel train from India in one hand. Now that he was in league with the fishermen, the market was also out of bounds for Ali.

3. Impossible Dreams

Ali ran until he reached the docklands, where he could finally let his guard down and breathe easy. He strolled out onto a familiar, rickety old wharf, and plonked down on the end of it, shooing away a beady-eyed crow. He let his bare feet dangle over the edge, the waves lapping at his toes, and let out a sigh. Seagulls screeched and wheeled overhead. He inhaled the sea air, ripe with brine and seaweed.

Behind him, a couple of waterfront brats, boys about ten or eleven years old, were skylarking on the wharf, laughing and jeering. He glanced around to see a skinny one with a mop of dark brown hair toss something black and furry off the side of the wharf.

It yowled in terror as it splashed into the water, and Ali realised it was a kitten.

A short, pudgy boy with a shaved head hooted and whooped, and threw a stone at the floundering animal.

"Hey, stop!" Ali yelled. He dropped his kebabs onto the salt-bleached wharf and lurched to his feet.

The boys glanced his way but paid him no heed, both now laughing and throwing stones at the terrified kitten.

Ali charged at them. He shoved the shorter one in the back and he pitched off the wharf with a startled cry. The other boy swung a wild punch at Ali, but he side-stepped the blow and cuffed him across the side of his head. The boy lost his balance and Ali kicked him in the bum, sending him nose-diving into the water to join his friend. Bobbing in the harbour, the cruel boys cursed him.

"Have some of your own medicine," Ali said.

He picked up a couple of the stones the boys had brought to torture the kitten, weighing one in his right hand. He took careful aim, and threw it at the brown-haired boy. Not too hard, because he was a good shot and he didn't want to do any serious damage, just teach him a lesson. The missile struck the boy on the side of the head with a *thud* and he yelped. Then Ali hurled the second stone at the other boy, hitting him on the shoulder.

The boys swore and bellowed, then paddled hurriedly towards the shore.

Ali dropped onto his belly, leaned over the edge of the wharf, and reached down with both hands. He caught hold of the struggling kitten and hoisted it out of the water. It was jet black, except for four white socks, a snowy patch on its face and belly, and a tiny pink nose. At first the sodden little thing hissed and scratched at him, but he cuddled it and carried it back to the end of the wharf where he sat down, waved buzzing flies from his now cold kebabs, and broke off a chunk of the fish for the bedraggled kitten.

Before long, it was purring softly in his arms.

Ali helped himself to one of the kebabs and took a bite. Cold as it was, the spiced swordfish pieces were still delicious and he relished every morsel. But before he had finished the first stick, he was startled by a skull-faced old man standing over him wearing an imposingly tall, black felt *kalpak* hat.

"Greetings, young Ali," the newcomer, a man called Fedar, said, wringing his bony hands together even though the day was not cold. "What's that you've got there, a drowned rat?"

Ali rolled his eyes.

Fedar reached his hand out to touch the kitten, but it arched its back and hissed, then jumped from Ali's lap and scurried back along the wharf. Ali peered anxiously after it, then relaxed when he saw it join a litter of other kittens mewling around their mother.

"Want a kebab?" Ali asked.

"You've always had a soft spot for animals and waifs," Fedar said, squinting after the kitten. "Since you were a toddler." He selected a kebab stick and squatted beside Ali, adjusting his long magenta cloak. "Will I be in trouble for eating this delicacy?"

"What do you mean?"

"I understand there is a very angry fat man in the bazaar today." Fedar gave a complicit snigger and devoured the spicy kebab pieces in two quick gulps, barely even chewing. He licked the thin wooden skewer clean and tossed it into the water. "I also hear there was an unfortunate incident at the beach this morning. I hear tell you had a strange dream and the fishermen are after you."

"*Nightmare*, you mean," Ali said. Then he gave Fedar a sharp look. "How do you know? And how did you find me here?"

The old man made a brushing-aside gesture with his hand. "Call it a good guess. What did you dream about?"

"I dreamed that tiger sharks attacked and killed Hasan the fisherman."

Fedar smirked knowingly. "The drunkard who gave you a beating when you accidentally spilled his cup in that waterfront taverna where you work?"

Something painful shifted in Ali's chest. "I tried to warn him, but he wouldn't listen."

"And I warned you about the risks of working there," Fedar said.

"It's honest money, Fedar." Ali met the old man's gaze. "Better than the cheating and stealing you taught me. I went to work there because I believe life has more in store for me than being your lackey, or living hand to mouth on the streets. I want more than that. I want to save some money, leave Korykos, and make a better life for myself. Perhaps even do some good in the world."

"How *very noble* of you," Fedar mocked. Then he sighed. "We've had this conversation many times already. I know it's one of the reasons you moved out of my house. But I didn't come here to dredge up old arguments, I came to talk about this dream you had. I know something of these kinds of dreams. Once you have had one, you will have more. They will plague you, weigh heavily on you."

Ali blew out his breath in exasperation. "Why did it happen

to me? I don't want any more dreams like that. It frightened me."

"It would be wise," Fedar said sternly, "for you to come back to stay with me again for a time. It will be better than living on the street and dossing down wherever you can find a bed. I can help you."

Ali peered into the old man's bloodshot eyes and remembered him asking questions about his dreams on other occasions. In fact, Fedar had shown more than a passing interest in Ali's dreams and nightmares for the last couple of years. The recollection of these interrogations made him suspicious.

"Can you truly stop me having any more dreams like that?" he asked cautiously.

Fedar leaned forward. "If that's what you want."

"Of course it's what I want."

"What if there was another option?" Fedar asked, stroking his long white beard. "A *better* option. What if your dreams come true only because *you* dream them? What if you are not merely predicting the future, but *creating* the future?"

Ali's jaw dropped. "That's impossible."

"Is it?" The old man reached across and gripped Ali's shoulder, his bony fingers digging into the soft flesh there. "Imagine if I could help you control the dreams, focus their energy. Instead of being nightmares they would be a powerful gift."

Ali's eyes grew wide.

Fedar's mouth curled in an almost sinister grin. "I could help and guide you... Just think of the possibilities, boy."

Ali shook his head and shrugged free of Fedar's grasp. "Forget about it. I just want them to stop. It was a weird nightmare. It left me feeling hollow and sick."

"Trust me," Fedar said, patting him on the forearm. "I've always had your best interests at heart, you know that. Why else would I have taken you in when your mother died?"

Ali thought about that. Fedar had adopted him when he was an orphaned infant. "Adopted" was probably too strong a word. He had given Ali a roof over his head: first in the cupboard behind the kitchen with Sara, Fedar's old housekeeper, who had mothered him, and whom Ali had loved; then in the tiny room over the stables after Sara had died from the black plague when Ali was about ten years old.

"Trust you? The person who schooled me in the arts of begging, cheating and thieving before you even taught me to read?"

"But I did teach you, Ali," Fedar said in a wheedling tone. "They are all skills that have served you well. Not only that, but I fed and clothed you. Without me you would have perished. I am the closest thing to a father you ever had, and probably the only person who can help you now." He tried to smile but it was more like a grimace. "Your one true friend."

Ali shut his eyes and pinched the bridge of his nose, his feelings and thoughts about Fedar conflicted. "What you say about my dreams sounds farfetched."

"Come home with me, Ali. If nothing else, I can protect you from the fishermen."

"I'll think about it," he said, a pained expression crossing his face.

"As you wish," Fedar said gruffly. He rose with the aid of his gnarled staff, turned and strode away.

Ali was left alone with his thoughts. What Fedar had proposed sounded fantastic, but what if it was true? What if his dreams were creating the future? He realised the horrible implication. That the fisher-folk were right and Ali was indeed responsible for killing Hasan.

4. The Peculiar Sailor

Walking along Crescent Moon Street, Ali stopped when a woman with a tasselled, pale-blue Romani scarf draped over her head called to him. She was standing in a roadside booth beneath a faded red canvas awning.

"Hear your future, young man?" she asked.

She was a fortune-teller and herbalist, one of the many self-styled pundits who plied their trade near the harbour. Many people believed the Romani were magicians, but she had a kind face so Ali stopped to look into her stall. His gaze travelled over the many stoppered bottles, jars and phials displayed on the trestle in front of her.

"A potion, perhaps?" Her long fingers, decorated with mystical henna tattoo designs, fluttered over her wares.

He shrugged. "Perhaps."

In the past, Ali had always gone to Fedar for potions when he needed them, but the conversation on the dock with the old man had troubled him. He didn't trust Fedar anymore. After constant disagreements and bickering with him, he had finally left Fedar's house two years ago. Before that, when he was younger, he used to look up to the old man, even thought of him as a father figure, but those days were long gone. Ali had learned from bitter experience that Fedar often had ulterior motives, and manipulated people to his own ends. Rather than go to him now, Ali decided to see if this gypsy could help.

"Do you have anything for dreams?" he asked.

"Poppy resin," she said. "Quite popular with a lot of the sailors.

It will send you straight to dreamland."

"No," he said. "That's not what I mean. I want to get rid of my dreams. I want to stop them, make them go away."

She studied him closely, her brow furrowed. "You have nightmares?"

"Something like that."

She scratched her head. "Not a common request. Young men usually seek love potions." She chuckled. "Or should I say lust potions. They want to get young women to accept their advances."

Colour rose in Ali's face. He shook his head. "Just something to stop my dreams."

She looked him up and down, taking in his skinny physique. "One drop under your tongue at bedtime should do the trick. A tincture of skullcap, dogwood and nightglory. But *only* one drop, else you'll regret it."

The Romani woman prepared the mixture and gave it to him in a small wood-stoppered terracotta phial. Ali handed over the last of his coppers in payment, hoping that the potion would work. Now in need of money for dinner and lodgings, he made his way back to the dock, twisting his leg and dragging his foot like a cripple.

"*Baksheesh*?" he cried to the sailors and women who spilled out of the boisterous tavernas and lurched along the cobbled streets.

Most people ignored him, but every so often someone tossed him a few coppers. Sailors on shore leave with money in their purses and Armenian wine in their bellies proved to be his greatest benefactors, and before long his purse jangled with the clink of loose change.

He fell into his begging routine again when he saw a grizzled, scruffy-bearded sailor approaching, but paused to stare in amazement when he realised the man had a rare gemeye—a luck bird, as they were popularly known—a stout bird, with a medium length tail, and a broad beak perched on his shoulder. Even this late in the afternoon the bird's iridescent metallic feathers glinted with rainbows of sunlight.

"*Baksheesh*, kind *efendi*?" Ali said almost as an afterthought, smitten by the presence of the bird.

The man stopped and scowled at him. The gemeye screeched, its emerald eyes ablaze with inner light.

"What are you doing?" the sailor asked gruffly.

"Begging." Ali took a limping step to demonstrate his supposed disability. "*Baksheesh,* kind *efendi*?"

"You are deceiving people," the grizzled sailor said. "There's nothing wrong with your leg. I saw you running along Crescent Moon Street not long ago. You're taking money under false pretences, money meant for people needier than yourself. Is such an act worthy of you?"

Ali felt his face flush hotly. Never before had he been confronted in this manner. He had often been accused of wrongdoings, of course, but this man was asking him to consider the morality of his behaviour.

"I need money too," he said defensively.

"Yes, I'm sure you do," the man said, his tone now a touch kindlier.

He spoke with a north-western accent, Ali thought. Perhaps from Edirne, the royal capital of all Anatolia, or even the old capital, Bursa.

"What's your name, boy?" the sailor asked.

He considered lying, but decided to tell the truth. "Ali."

"Do you have a family name?"

Ali shrugged. In truth he did not know. He had asked Fedar about his mother and father on numerous occasions, but the old man had evaded giving a real answer, telling him he knew nothing of his father or family.

"I'm looking for a youth about sixteen years old," the sailor said. "You might be him, but either way, if you'll answer some questions I'll make it worth your while."

"The same age as me, but I doubt I'm the one you seek," Ali said.

The sailor smiled kindly. "Maybe not, but you might know him."

"What's his name?" Ali asked.

"Yusuf," the sailor said.

Ali relaxed, shaking his head. "Don't know anyone around here by that name."

"What were your mother and father called?" the sailor asked.

"I don't know," Ali admitted. "I'm an orphan. My mother was a widow and she died when I was born."

The gemeye chirped and its eyes glowed more softly, sparkling with highlights. The sailor tilted his head closer to the bird, listening to it, then he turned his attention back to Ali.

"Do you have dreams, lad?"

A chill ran down Ali's spine and the hairs on the back of his neck stood up. He felt suddenly cold, despite the warmth of the day. How could this peculiar sailor possibly know about his dreams?

"Everybody has dreams," he said guardedly.

The sailor fixed him with a piercing gaze "But not everybody has extraordinary dreams."

Ali glanced around for a means of escape, his heart racing. "I don't know what you're talking about."

"Perhaps," the sailor said. "In any case, I have some advice for you. Wicked men covet the kind of power I am talking about. If you have extraordinary dreams, be wary of those who offer you help. They may be in league with evil forces."

All of a sudden, the gemeye gave a loud screech and launched itself from the sailor's shoulder. It darted straight at a large black crow that had appeared on the edge of the roof above them.

The crow squawked in alarm and took off, disappearing over the rooftops with the gemeye in hot pursuit. A minute or so later the gemeye circled back and alighted once again on the sailor's shoulder, where it chirped whisper-like into his ear.

The sailor grimaced. "There are men coming. I must go."

"What men?" Ali asked, fearing they were the fishermen who'd been pursuing him.

The sailor reached out and gripped his arm. "Seek Luman for guidance to help deal with the burden I suspect you carry. Others may assist or hinder in their own way, but only Luman can truly give you succour."

Ali frowned. "But he is a myth. I know people still pray to him, but he's just a legendary saint. Gone the way of Tengri and the old beliefs. How can I seek him?"

"I must go," the sailor said. "The men looking for me are almost here. You will be safe if you wait quietly behind the taverna over there until they have passed."

"You said you would make it worth my while if I answered your questions," Ali reminded him.

The hint of a smile revealed itself at the corner of the sailor's mouth. He pulled out a purse, and shook a handful of coins into Ali's outstretched palm.

"Thank you," Ali said gratefully when he saw a pair of silver *akçes* glinting amongst the coppers.

"Now go," the sailor said, giving him a gentle shove. "Remember what I said. Be wary and seek Luman."

Ali dropped the coins into his purse and crossed to the rear of the taverna. The sailor hurried away along the cobbled street, pausing briefly at the end to give Ali a small wave. The eyes of the gemeye on his shoulder flashed with emerald sparks, then the man turned the corner and they were gone.

Ali waited quietly like he was told, not only because of the sailor's earnestness, but also because he still feared the men coming might be the fishermen. Before long there came the sound of booted feet on the cobbles and a group of heavily armed Uzbegs brandishing war clubs and axes hurried past.

5. A Luck Coin and the Potion

It was sunset and the müezzin's *ezan* echoed in the distance, calling the Muslim faithful to prayer. Ali came out from behind the taverna and headed in the opposite direction to the way the Uzbegs had gone, making his way to the caravanserai near the waterfront.

Thoughts tumbled in confusion through his head as he walked. Should he trust the peculiar sailor? Or was his generosity a form of seduction? Could he put any trust at all in Fedar? He was already wary of him, but something about his manner, his urgency and hunger about Ali's dream, made him even more uncomfortable.

Ali did not know what to do or who to trust, but at least he should be safe for the night in the caravanserai. It was a haven for traders and travellers alike, built like a fortress, with an open inner courtyard surrounded by high, thick stone walls that could only be accessed through a single gated entrance. On the ground level around the inside wall there were animal pens, stables and other chambers. Above them were bedrooms, bathrooms and a cheap but hearty inn where he was known and welcome, as long as he paid his way.

It was already dark when he arrived. The gateman recognised him and let him in. Ali crossed the central quadrangle to the gurgling fountain in the middle of the yard, and stood there quietly for a few minutes, watching and listening.

Occasionally a camel grunted or bellowed from one of their pens, or a horse nickered in the stables, but otherwise all was dark and silent except for a flicker of lamplight coming from the small mosque in the far corner. On the upper level the murmur of voices came from some of the apartments. Then the door of the inn above the stables flew open. Light shone, revealing a sailor who cried his farewells and staggered to his sleeping quarters.

Nothing appeared untoward. Ali climbed the narrow wooden stairs to the inn and went inside. He took a seat on a stool at the rough-hewn bar. At the end of the bar a nut-brown old man played a popular sailors' work song on a battered *baglama,* nursing its gourd-like body on his lap, fingers making familiar chords along the neck as he strummed with the other hand.

Ali glanced around the room.

A few other patrons sat quietly at benches drinking Albanian wine or Bulgarian ale and playing *tavla,* a backgammon-like board game.

The innkeeper cocked a quizzical eyebrow at Ali.

"A stable bed for the night," Ali said. "Plus some of your excellent *gozleme.* My stomach is grumbling just thinking about it."

"Cash up front," the innkeeper said in a genial but no-nonsense way.

Ali dug in his purse for one of the silver *akçe* coins the peculiar sailor had given him and laid it on the bar with a flourish.

The innkeeper furrowed his brow as he took the coin. Then his eyes went suddenly wide. "God's mercy!" he said. "This is a luck coin!"

"Huh?" Ali snatched it back.

He was right. It was not an *akçe,* but a rare luck coin. More valuable even than a pure silver Byzantine *stavraton.* But its real worth was the purported good fortune it bestowed on its owner. Ali quickly slipped it back into his purse and retrieved the other silver coin, an ordinary *akçe,* and offered it instead.

The innkeeper carefully examined the coin before calling Ali's order to the kitchenette. A wizened old woman with wisps of grey hair poking out from under the faded blue scarf tied over her head nodded and set to work. She used a narrow wooden pin to roll out a chunk of dough until it was almost paper thin. Then she sprinkled it with a mix of crumbly white cheese, chopped spinach, garlic and olive oil before folding the pastry into a flat envelope and tossing it onto a wood-fired griddle to fry.

"Never seen a luck coin before," the innkeeper said, counting Ali's change back into his open hand.

Ali put the coins away in his purse and, not taking any chances, took his plate of hot *gozleme* to an inconspicuous bench in the back corner of the inn. There, he could sit and keep an eye on the comings and goings while he ate his meal.

But he couldn't stop thinking about the luck coin.

Who would have thought? Did the peculiar sailor know he had given him a luck coin? If so, why would he give him such a precious gift? Thinking about the sailor made Ali wonder how the man knew about his dreams, and what his ambiguous warning meant.

Ali rubbed a hand through his hair. Was the sailor trying to warn him about Fedar?

Surely not.

Seek Luman, the sailor had said. What kind of advice was that? Luman was a legend. Sure, people prayed to him, many thought him a saint, whether for the old god Tengri or one of the Muslim or Christian sects. But only fanatics and lunatics went looking for him. Ali let out his breath in a long, slow sigh. Now he was more confused than ever.

He licked his fingertips and dabbed his plate to pick up the last of the pastry and cheese crumbs, rose from his seat and let himself out of the inn. As he climbed down to the courtyard, the moon illuminated his way. He crossed to the stables beneath the inn, his footsteps quiet on the compacted earth. Inside, he squeezed between the horses, whispered soothing words to them, and climbed into the loft behind the inn. There, he found a spare horse blanket and made a comfortable bed in the straw.

Now that he was alone, Ali took the luck coin from his purse and examined it in a patch of pale moonlight slanting into the loft. He rubbed it between his fingers. It was minted with the raised image of a luck bird on one face and an unusual spiral maze-like pattern on the other. He ran a finger across the spiral pattern, realising it was a puzzle with false turns and dead ends, but he quickly found the right path to the centre of the maze. The coin felt comforting, smooth and warm to his touch. Someone had punched a small hole through the edge of it so it could be threaded on a thong or string and worn as an amulet.

He returned it to his purse and tucked the purse safely beneath his waist sash. Then he took out the small terracotta phial he had purchased from the Romani woman on Crescent Moon Street. With any luck this potion would solve his problems. He pulled the wooden stopper, screwed up his nose at the evil-smelling concoction, and tipped a drop of it under his tongue.

"*Ughh*!" It tasted like cat's piss.

He wanted to spit it out but instead braced himself and, despite the Romani woman's warning, poured a few more drops into his mouth to make certain.

He put the phial away and made himself comfortable using an old sack filled with straw for a pillow. Snuggled there in the hay of the loft, the closest thing to a bed he had seen for over a week, Ali dropped off to sleep, exhausted.

He slept peacefully until the early hours of the morning when he began to dream. A ruby-tinged dream…

Ali dreamed of a blue-and-white-striped stall in the bazaar with a fat, turbaned man at work within. It was Big-hands, using his cleaver to chop a large piece of swordfish into chunks, scraping the pieces from the chopping block into an earthenware bowl of olive oil and spices.

Then the kebab man turned his attention to the firebox of his char, filling it with firewood in preparation for the breakfast rush. He ignited the kindling and when the logs were well alight, burning down to form a fiery glow of coals, he resumed his chopping.

Then trouble struck.

Ali saw it in his mind's eye in slow motion.

Big-hands swung his cleaver, but was distracted when a blazing log fell from the fire. He twisted aside, taking his eyes away from the chopping block. But the cleaver was still in motion and it came down and bit into human flesh and bone.

The man screamed.

Ali woke trembling, his heart racing, his hair plastered to his face, his body slick and sticky with cold sweat. There was a bitter, coppery taste in his mouth. His stomach heaved and he retched, vomiting the half-digested remains of his dinner into the straw, replacing the coppery taste in his mouth with that of the vile potion he had taken at bedtime.

Fat lot of good the dreadful stuff had done him.

He vomited over and over until he was dry retching, before falling back limp, drained and spent. He lay there like that for the rest of the night, too weak to move, listening to the sounds of the stable animals below farting, grunting and stirring in their sleep.

When the first rays of dawn light slanted through the cracks in the roof and walls of the loft and a rooster crowed nearby, Ali tried to rise but the attempt made his head spin and he collapsed again, exhausted.

It was mid-morning by the time he felt well enough to rise. Too late to warn Big-hands, he thought dejectedly. But he had to try anyway, despite the risks.

He climbed down from the loft on shaky legs and dragged himself to the Old City. He kept his eyes open, fearful of meeting an angry fisherman. In his sickly, light-headed state, he would have trouble outrunning an old man, let alone a fit and healthy one.

When he reached the bazaar, he skirted around a cart heaped with ripe, green-skinned melons from Persia, past wicker baskets spilling over with green, pink and purple late-season grapes, and across the sun-bleached square to the lane where Big-hands plied his trade.

Even as he approached the kebab stall Ali knew it was empty; the familiar smoky, spiced aroma of the place was missing. Sure enough, the stall was unmanned and on closer examination he noticed several broken kebab sticks lying in the blood-spattered dust.

Suddenly dizzy, Ali reached out and grabbed the bare serving counter to steady himself.

"You won't get no kebab today," a female voice said.

He turned to see the gossipy woman from a nearby sweetmeats stall standing there.

"Unbelievable," she said. "Big-hands chopped off his fingers with a cleaver." She gave a wry chuckle. "His hand ain't so big now."

Ali choked a sob and slid to the dusty ground. Fedar might be right. Ali was not only responsible for Hasan's death, but now Big-hands had lost his fingers because of him.

He felt miserable. Guilty and responsible.

The sweetmeats stall woman shrugged and went on her way.

6. The Slave Girl

It was late afternoon before Ali's strength returned and he felt well enough to eat something. He managed to sip a cup of honey water and nibble a piece of cold flatbread, then made his way to the docks.

Ali ignored the busy waterside workers calling and yammering to each other. He skirted around them as they lugged sacks bulging with salt, loaded wagons with clay jars of olive oil, and manhandled barrels of wine and honey. He found a place to sit on an upright barrel, where the cool sea breeze on his face had a soothing effect.

He was fiddling with the luck coin the peculiar sailor had given him, when he noticed a sleek galley built of cedar and gum arabic timber—singularly different to the usual cargo ships and ferries that plied these waters—cutting swiftly across the harbour. Its upper deck was decorated with fretwork, coloured pennants fluttered on the two-masted rigging, and it was crewed by foreign, dark-skinned men.

Ali jumped from his perch and hurried along the quayside to get a closer view of it as it docked. The galley was a Barbary slaver, come to replenish supplies en route to the İskenderūn slave market. Sailors lowered the gangplank and began to oversee the loading of provisions. Workers lined up with wicker baskets heaped with fruit and vegetables balanced on their heads, while brawny stevedores lugged heavy barrels and crates on board.

Suddenly there was a commotion back along the wharf.

"Stop that girl," someone yelled. "Little bitch! Don't let her escape."

Ali turned to see a pretty teenage girl running headlong in his direction. Behind her a pair of brawny thugs were in hot pursuit. Ali admired her guts and determination, but there was little hope of escape because she had run the wrong way and was heading for the end of the wharf.

The girl gave Ali a quick glance, her almond-shaped eyes, as green as new spring growth, meeting his own for the briefest moment, and he saw she was not just pretty but was strikingly beautiful.

"Watch out!" Ali called, pointing.

The girl realised her mistake and skidded to a halt at the end of the wharf. Tottering there, the sunlight shone through her simple cheesecloth kaftan. Ali glimpsed the outline of her lithe body through the thin fabric and his pulse began to race.

But his momentary thrill turned to outrage as the girl's pursuers ran her down. She kicked, thrashed and scratched, but the brutish pair quickly overpowered her. They twisted one of her arms behind her back until a swarthy man dressed in gaudy silks caught them up.

The silk-clad man slapped the girl's face.

"Careful of the merchandise, worm!" commanded a foreign-accented voice.

The speaker stood resplendent at the prow of the slave galley. He was a grey-bearded black man dressed in long, baggy indigo-blue pants caught in at the ankle and tied at the waist with a red sash, and a cherry-coloured waistcoat trimmed with gold brocade over an amber vest. His arms were scarred with battle marks and he tapped on the hilt of his low-slung scimitar.

"That girl is more valuable than your life is worth," he said coldly. "My master will ensure you pay dearly if she is marked or defiled."

In response, the swarthy man snatched a handful of the girl's short, raven-black hair, pulled her free of his henchmen, and yanked her head back. She whimpered in submission, tears running afresh down her already reddened cheeks. Then he ripped the kaftan she wore off one shoulder, exposing a small, brown-nippled breast.

"Look at her," he said. "A virgin, not a mark on her. I have done exactly as ordered. Now she is your problem."

The girl cowered in fear and humiliation, desperately trying to clutch the torn pieces of her kaftan back together with her free hand.

"Bring her aboard then," growled the slaver captain.

Ali glared in indignation as the man in gaudy silks dragged the defenceless girl stumbling towards the gangplank. "Let her go," he shouted, his body tense, his muscles quivering.

The man halted and turned to look Ali up and down. Then his lip curled in a sneer and he yanked the girl forward again.

She stumbled and gave a sob.

Ali planted his feet wide and bared his teeth, casting about for something to throw, but found nothing. Then his gaze fell on the coin in his hand and without a moment's thought he threw it at the man with all the force he could muster.

The coin whizzed through the air and struck the swarthy man on the back of his head. He bellowed in surprise and anger, released his grip on the slave girl, who crumpled to the weathered dock, and snatched a whip from a nearby slaver.

But before the man could even uncoil the whip, Ali leaped off the wharf. He hit the water in a shallow dive and surfaced to find the silk-clad man leaning over the edge shaking his fist and spitting curses at him.

Ali had a sinking feeling in his stomach when he realised he had thrown his luck coin in the heat of the moment. He glanced back at the wharf in despair.

The slave girl had scrambled unnoticed to the end of the wharf, and taking Ali's lead, she too flung herself into the harbour. She went under and did not reappear. The whip-wielder jumped to his feet and roared with fury. Ali swam into the shadows beneath the wharf, guessing the girl had sought refuge there, but there was no sign of her. Then she suddenly burst to the surface beside him and flung her arms around his neck.

"Help me," she pleaded.

Ali could feel her body pressed against his, her heart thumping against his chest. He looked desperately around for some means of escape. Beyond the wharf lay the open harbour. On one side of them the slave galley gently bumped and nudged the pylons, while along the other side of the wharf smaller craft bobbed at the ends of their mooring ropes. Overhead there was a commotion on the dock, shouts and running feet.

"Quick," she said. "We can hide over there between those boats."

Ali shook his head. "They'll find us there." Then an idea came to him and he grinned. "Can you swim?" he asked.

The girl nodded vigorously. "I can make it to the island," she said, looking out to sea, to the harbour entry. "We can hide in the fortress there."

"The Maiden's Castle," Ali said. "No, they'd catch us before we could reach it. And even if we did make it to the island we'd be trapped there. I've got another idea. Follow me."

He struck out swiftly for the harbour shore, swimming directly beneath the wharf towards the mainland. The girl swam with him, matching him stroke for stroke. But at the shoreline they came to a halt, their way blocked by a sandstone seawall rising from the harbour bed.

"Where to now?" she said in alarm.

Ali shushed her and groped along the wall.

"It smells horrible under here," the girl complained.

Someone above them yelled, "They're under the wharf."

Then Ali's fingers located a drain outlet high on the quayside wall and he hauled himself into its dark mouth. The girl gasped as he disappeared inside, but grinned broadly when he reappeared in the opening and reached down to pull her after him into the dank interior.

"Yuck!" she complained, her expression quickly turning into a grimace of disgust. "It stinks in here."

Outside, men were splashing about in the water.

"Over 'ere," a rough voice said.

Ali dragged the girl behind him, sliding on hands and knees through the slimy, fetid water in the bottom of the drain. Soon the sounds of pursuit faded to silence behind them and they found themselves completely shrouded in pitch-black darkness.

"Where are you taking me?" the girl whispered.

"This drain leads to a tunnel that runs down from the castle, the fortress that overlooks and protects the city. I think it was used as a secret escape route in the old days. It's pretty much forgotten now."

"This is revolting," she said.

Ali smiled to himself. "Hopefully that's what our pursuers will think, too."

They crawled on through shallow sludgy water, deeper and deeper into the drain beneath Korykos, navigating by touch along the slimy stone walls.

Suddenly there was a *plop* in the water ahead.

"What was that?" the girl asked.

"Probably a rat," Ali said.

"I'm not going any further," she said with finality.

"All it wants to do is get out of our way. It won't try to bite unless we corner it. Just follow me."

They felt their way in single file through the coal-pit blackness, until the drain they were navigating intersected with a larger tunnel. Ali turned into the right-hand fork and paused while the girl came alongside him.

"There's a place a bit further ahead where we'll be safe," he said.

"How do you know?"

Ali chuckled. "I used to hunt rats under here when I was a kid."

"A man of many talents," she said wryly. "What's your name?"

"Ali. What's yours?"

"Call me Rose," she said. She groped in the dark for his hand and gave it a squeeze. "Thank you, Ali."

He felt his face flush. "We'd better keep moving," he said awkwardly.

They pressed on until eventually there was a faint light ahead, and soon the tunnel they were passing through opened into a large rectangular chamber, light filtering down from somewhere high above.

Ali dropped to the bottom of the pit and sank to his ankles

in thick, dark sludge. He steadied himself and held his arms up. "Come on," he said, motioning to her. "Jump."

Rose wrinkled her nose. "I'm not jumping down there."

"I'll catch you," he said. "It's the only way out."

"Where?" she asked, looking around and seeing a scaffold of rickety wooden stairs zig-zagging up the side of the pit. "Up those?"

He shook his head. "They used to lead to the fortress, but they're rotten and broken now and the way further ahead is blocked by fallen masonry." He pointed to a heavy wooden grate in the ceiling of the chamber. "We have to go up there."

She craned her neck. "How do we do that?"

"There are hand- and footholds in the bricks. We'll have to climb."

She swallowed.

"But not for a few hours," he added. "We need to wait until dark. Less chance of being seen. Jump down to me and I'll carry you across to the other side where there's a place we can sit and wait."

Rose took a deep breath, and jumped.

But her fall caught Ali off balance and he slipped, tumbling back into the mire. She landed awkwardly on top of him, and they found themselves pressed face to face. Rose squirmed in an attempt to disentangle herself, and Ali tried to push her up.

Rose's eyes shot wide open and she slapped him hard across the face.

Ali gasped, realising he had inadvertently clutched her bare breast. He let go in alarm, only to have her fall straight back on top of him.

Rose scrambled inelegantly to her feet and wrenched the damp, limp pieces of her torn kaftan back together in an attempt to cover herself. She gave him a defiant glare.

"Sorry," Ali said, his face burning with embarrassment. "It was an accident, truly."

"You look ridiculous lying there in the muck," she said, shaking her head, an amused smile on her lips.

Ali blinked at this unexpected response and struggled to his feet. The sludge made a wet, sucking sound as he pulled himself free. He removed his damp, muck-grimed vest, shook it out and did his best to brush it clean.

"You better have this," he said, offering it to her.

She hesitated, an expression of distaste on her face, then seized it from him. He waited while she draped the sorry garment around herself, then he led her in silence to a broad brick ledge on the other side of the chamber.

"I thought you were going to carry me," Rose said in mock petulance, slumping back against the wall and kicking sludge from her feet.

"We kind of got distracted," Ali said sheepishly, taking a seat nearby.

Rose scraped the worst of the caked filth from her legs, then tried to rub her fingers clean on the bricks before wiping her face.

"How do I look?" she asked.

Beautiful, Ali thought, despite her grubby, dishevelled appearance. He could hardly look at her for fear his heart would stop. She looked like a goddess.

"Better than me," he managed. He got to his feet and walked to the other end of the pit, where he made a pretence of examining the wall. He already knew where the hand- and footholds were, but he was unsettled and didn't know what to say to this girl.

They lapsed into silence.

"Why is the fortress on the island in the bay called the Maiden's Castle?" she said at last.

"According to the legend," Ali said, "a sultan who lived here in the mainland fortress in olden times had a beautiful daughter. But when she was born, the palace soothsayer foretold she would die from a snake bite on her sixteenth birthday."

"What happened to her?"

"To protect her the sultan had that castle built for her on the little island so she could live there in safety. But on her sixteenth birthday, a snake sneaked into the stronghold hidden in a basket of fruit brought for her from the mainland. It bit her and she died."

"Oh, that's sad," Rose said. "It sounds like a story from *One Thousand and One Nights*. She was so young, the same age I'll be on my next birthday."

"Lucky you're not a princess with a birth prophecy hanging over your head," he said, realising she was just a little younger than he was.

She didn't respond. Ali felt her eyes on him and turned back to face her.

"Why are you helping me, Ali?" Her green-eyed gaze searched his. "Surely it's dangerous for you."

"I hate to see a beautiful lady in distress," he said flippantly.

She gave a sad smile. "But now they will be hunting for you too."

Ali gave a sardonic snort. "They can get in line. There are enough people in this city hunting for me already."

"Then you might need this," she said, handing him a silver coin.

Ali's eyebrows rose in surprise and he took it from her. "My luck coin... How—"

"I snatched it off the dock when you jumped into the water. It was lucky for me, so I carried it with me through the drain. I hope it will be lucky for you, too."

"Thanks," he said, returning it to his purse. "Let's hope it's lucky for both of us." He looked at the grate above them. "It's getting dark. We should leave while we can still see the foot- and handholds. We can hide in the bushes up there until it's full dark."

Rose gripped his arm. "I'm scared, Ali. What if they're up there?"

"They won't be. Hardly anyone knows about this place." He prised her fingers loose and gave them a gentle, reassuring squeeze.

"What if I fall?" she asked.

"You won't fall," he said. "Just follow me and watch what I do. It's easier than what you did crawling through the drain to get here."

Ali scaled the wall of the chamber, showing her where each foot-and-handhold was as they went. At the top he paused and listened for a minute, then thrust open the wooden grate. It fell away with a thud and Ali poked his head out into fresh air.

It was twilight. They were surrounded by thick, aromatic

juniper bushes, effectively hiding them from view. A light breeze was blowing. Birds were chirping in nearby trees, preparing for sleep, and a dog barked somewhere, but otherwise the evening seemed calm. He clambered out and turned back to help Rose.

She joined him with a look of relief, but then her eyes went suddenly wide.

Ali spun around.

A large shape loomed out of the dark bushes.

Something swished through the air.

His head whipped back, fireworks exploded behind his eyes and everything went black.

7. In Fedar's Clutches

Ali came half-awake and tried to swim towards consciousness. His head thumped. The air was filled with the cloying odour of noisome chemicals. He sensed movement and squeezed his eyes open a crack, but everything was a blur.

A voice that was familiar said, "So you are awake."

Ali groaned. He felt as though a squad of guardsmen had beaten him senseless with hardwood cudgels. Who knows, maybe that's what had happened to him.

Then he began to remember…

"Rose…" It was little more than a hoarse croak.

"What were you thinking?" scolded the voice.

"F-Fedar?" Ali said. "Is that you? Where's Rose?"

"The girl?"

Ali gave a feeble blink.

"Bound for the İskenderūn slave market, of course," Fedar said. "The same thing that would have happened to you had I not intervened."

Ali tried to sit, but his head whirled sickeningly and he collapsed, sliding back into the dark folds of unconsciousness.

He dreamed of Rose. Not a red-tinged prophetic dream, but a sweat-soaked nightmare in which he kept trying to save her from a series of bizarre dream creatures, only to fail each time. When he woke, he was weighed down by a crushing sense of loss, guilt and despair.

A beaded curtain rattled and Ali turned his head to find Fedar sweeping back into the room. He came over to Ali and felt his forehead with a chemical-stained hand.

"I'll mix something to help you feel better," Fedar said, but there was little compassion in his bedside manner. He went across to a bench stacked high with bubbling apparatus and measured a variety of powders into a flask of milky liquid.

Ali looked around the room. He had been installed on a swayback leather divan in a windowless room. This was not the tiny cupboard behind the kitchen or the little room over the stables he had occupied in Fedar's house when he was younger, but the old man's workroom where he conducted his experiments and produced his potions.

Fedar grunted with satisfaction and shuffled back across the small room. He put a flask to Ali's lips. "Here, drink some of this."

Ali sipped at the mixture. It had a bitter, metallic taste and he shuddered.

"The potion will take effect shortly," Fedar said.

Ali raised himself on one elbow, but slipped back again. "I have to find Rose," he groaned.

Fedar ignored him and returned to his work bench.

Ali closed his eyes but images of Hasan the fisherman, the peculiar sailor, Big-hands, a procession of Uzbegs, and the swarthy silk-clad man on the dock, all cavorted through his head in pursuit of Rose.

He opened his eyes and stared at the beeswax candle in the wrought iron sconce on the wall above him. Before long, its flickering flame became everything, dispelling his weird imaginings and concern for Rose, filling his entire consciousness. He could taste the scent of it, pungent and sickly sweet, like burnt honey. He could hear the rustle of the capering flame, the *plop, plop* sound of the hot wax dripping.

Then the range of this newfound sensitivity expanded beyond the candle. With every slight movement he made, the divan gave guttural groans and creaks, like a living thing. The air around him took on a downy, soft texture, as he imagined a cloud might feel, and he could taste its cool living flavour with each breath he took.

A lump that he could not swallow away rose in his throat, and hallucinations surreptitiously appeared around him, quickly overtaking reality. His watery gaze followed a parade of mutant flowers, outlandish creatures, and impossible geometric patterns dancing about the room.

Then a dark shape suddenly loomed over him.

"I am here to help you," Fedar said from far, far away. "You have come to seek my aid and I am treating you for your dreams…"

Ali tried to shake his head, but he felt helpless, unable to stave off Fedar's intrusion into his mind. He could feel the skull-faced old man imposing his will on him, but in Ali's disoriented, highly receptive state, he was unable to resist. The potion that Fedar had given him had sapped his will, his grasp on reality.

Fedar's assault continued until Ali was completely drained and barely conscious. The last thing he heard was the rattle of the bead curtain and the sound of Fedar's footsteps receding along the hall, then he slipped into a deep, dreamless sleep.

Ali woke with a start. The room was dark except for a muddy light coming from somewhere beyond the bead-curtained doorway. He sat up, shivering, and peered about. He was alone. He wondered how long he had been confined here in Fedar's workroom, unsure whether it had been hours or days.

He strained hard, trying to remember what had been happening to him, trying to part the haze that fogged his mind. He knew that Fedar had saved him from the slavers who'd attacked him and Rose when they emerged from the drains, but that was all. Gradually it came to him that he had participated in another session with Fedar—the latest of several—but like the previous occasions, Ali could not recall any of the details.

He stretched and slid off the divan, dropping quietly to the cold stone floor. The sound of muffled voices came from beyond the room and he padded barefoot to the doorway, but for some reason he came to an abrupt halt, unable to leave the room.

A feeling of sickness swept over him at the mere thought of stepping through the door, and did not abate until he dismissed the idea of leaving from his mind.

He peered through the beaded curtain. Fedar was at the other end of the hallway engaged in a hushed conversation with an unsavoury-looking, heavily bearded Uzbeg wearing a chainmail shirt and lamellar armour on his shoulders and upper arms. It was the same man Ali had seen on the street when he was running away from the angry mob of fishermen after Hasan's hapless death.

At the mention of his name, Ali pricked his ears; something about the tone of their voices urged him to remain hidden and quiet.

Fedar said, "Ali has no idea of the power he possesses. He thinks his dreams are precognitive. He doesn't know he's actually creating the future by dreaming it."

Ali gasped quietly. So, it was true.

The stranger's Tajiki Persian-accent rose. "But if you don't come with me to spring the trap on Erkan there might be trouble. We need your talents to subdue him."

"Shhh," Fedar hissed. "Keep your voice down, Khasis." He glanced over his shoulder but did not see Ali lurking at the door of the workroom. "It's a good plan," Fedar went on. "All you have to do is spring the trap." He stabbed his pointed finger into the other man's chest. "Don't mess it up."

"Prince Savich will expect you to be there," Khasis said angrily.

Who is Prince *Savich?* Ali wondered. *He wasn't one of Sultan Bayezid's sons, was he?*

"I have to stay here for now," Fedar said. "Ali is our best chance. I have been nurturing him for years, waiting to see if he would inherit his father's dreams. Now that it has finally happened, I have to take advantage. The boy trusts me and thinks I'm helping him." He sniggered. "I'm like a father to him."

Inherited his father's dreams… Ali reeled. *His* father. Fedar had lied. He knew who Ali's father was. Knew why he was experiencing these dreams.

Khasis stifled a snort.

Ali's jaw clenched. *Fedar must think me a fool,* he thought. There had been a time when Ali looked up to him, but those days were long gone. Now all he felt for the old man was mistrust and contempt.

"Well, that's what the boy thinks," Fedar said. "And now the investment is about to pay off. Tonight, I intend to test my ability to control his dreams. You go to İskenderūn and I'll follow in a day or so, depending on what happens here."

"What will I tell Savich?" asked Khasis.

"Tell him what I just told you! If I can gain control of Ali's dreams and use him to help Savich, he will be unstoppable. The throne will be his and we will get our rewards. Now leave me. I have to rekindle Ali's dreams in preparation for the experiment. After that he will either be ours, or..." Fedar shrugged. "There's really no choice, Khasis. Either Ali will be in my power or the treatment will kill him."

Ali staggered. His legs turned to jelly. He grabbed the door-frame to steady himself.

Khasis poked his finger into Fedar's skull-like face. "I hope you know what you're doing. You're playing with fire. If I were you, I would pray to God that the boy doesn't turn those dreams against you."

"Do you think me a fool?" Fedar snapped. "I am controlling Ali with a potent combination of hypnosis, drugs and sorcery. Even after I unbind his dreams he cannot use them against me. I've seen to that."

"But what if he escapes?" Khasis asked.

"He cannot," Fedar insisted. "He is bound to my workroom. The only way he can leave is by submitting to my will. Either that or in a shroud."

"The same way his mother left when Savich had finished with her," Khasis said, sneering.

"It was the son Savich wanted, not the mother," Fedar said. "She had no dreaming potential. If all goes well, Ali will become Savich's puppet. A very powerful puppet."

Ali gagged on bile. He edged away from the door and stumbled on weak legs back to the divan. He slumped there with his shoulders drooping, his face in his hands. Finally, the truth was out. Fedar had known about his mother's murder. He had deceived and betrayed Ali all these years while he waited for him to start dreaming. Now Fedar was planning to use him, to use the power of his dreams—somehow inherited from his unknown father—to aid someone called Savich, his mother's murderer.

Blood was pounding so loudly in Ali's ears that he could barely contain his rage. He ground his teeth, clenching and unclenching his fists. The peculiar sailor had been right. Ali should never have trusted Fedar. He had been such a fool. He choked back a despairing sob. The fishermen had been right to blame him for Hasan's death. He was responsible for both that and for Bighands' accident.

This knowledge weighed heavily on Ali, but at the same time another fear rose in his mind. Fear that if Fedar were to gain control of his dreams, there was no telling what evil ends his future-shaping dream powers might be put to.

He could not let that happen. He took some slow deep breaths to calm himself.

One way or another, he had to find a way to stop Fedar and escape. He surveyed the room once more, but the only way out was through the door with the beaded curtain. He got unsteadily to his feet and tiptoed barefoot across to it, but when he reached it the same weird thing happened as last time. He came to a halt, as if he had run into an invisible wall.

The sound of heavy, plodding footsteps reached Ali's ears, and he stepped back out of sight as Sweyn, Fedar's gorilla-like manservant, shambled past. When he was gone, Ali moved back to the door and peered out. Fedar and Khasis were no longer in the hallway, so he tried to push his way through the curtain.

A wave of nausea swamped him. He fell to his knees, his head thumping, and crawled back to the divan. Escape through the door was impossible. Fedar had seen to that. But what other choices did he have?

Perhaps he could overcome Fedar. He would kill him if he had to—after all, not only had the old man admitted to keeping Ali prisoner all these years, he'd been party to the murder of Ali's mother.

Ali had never condoned murder in any circumstances, but was it murder to kill a murderer? Or was it justice? He sighed. When he thought about it, it felt more like revenge. He sat on the edge of the divan and licked his lips. He could not do it. His goal was to escape, not seek vengeance.

He got back to his feet and studied Fedar's workbench, looking for some sort of weapon. Anything: a knife, something to use as a club… But the only candidates were pieces of the old man's glass apparatus. Ali picked up a flask, planning to smash it and use the jagged end as a dagger. But the moment he thought about attacking Fedar, a sharp pain stabbed his gut, doubling him over, bitter, burning vomit rising in the back of his throat.

Ali dropped back on the divan in despair. Fedar had thought of everything. Ali was trapped and powerless. Even worse, Fedar was going to take control of him, of his future-shaping dreams, use him like a puppet. Then a thought struck him. A dark thought, but a possible solution to his predicament. If he played along with Fedar's plan, he just might be able to turn it against him. It would be a dire outcome for Ali himself, but it might be the only way to thwart the old man.

Fedar pushed through the beaded curtain carrying a lighted candle. He halted abruptly when he found Ali sitting up awake and scrutinised the boy suspiciously.

"What's wrong, Ali?" he asked.

Ali did his best to hide his fear and loathing, but he felt cold inside, chilled to his soul. "I…I don't know," he stammered. "Something woke me. Voices, I think."

Fedar narrowed his eyes and peered even harder at him.

Ali met his gaze and forced a thin smile.

Fedar tilted his head, weighing up the situation. "There was, ah…a visitor. Never mind, I was about to wake you anyway. The time is nigh, Ali. I believe you are ready to attempt a controlled dream."

Fedar placed the candle in the wrought-iron sconce on the wall above the divan where Ali was sitting and moved across the room to his workbench.

"I'm going to give you a sleeping potion." Fedar poured a milky liquid from a flask into a beaker, which he brought back to Ali. "It will make your slumber more conducive to dreaming."

Ali took the beaker without daring to speak lest his voice reveal his true feelings. He drained the chalky potion in a single gulp.

Fedar took back the empty beaker. "Lie down." He leaned over Ali's face and whispered dryly, "The potion will also leave your subconscious open to suggestion. You will hear and understand me not only when you are asleep, but also when you are dreaming."

Ali glared at the old man for a moment, then closed his eyes.

The potion took effect within minutes and Ali felt his consciousness slip away. But as the sleeping draught took hold, he fought back. He had heard Fedar say that the only way he could leave was by submitting to his will or in a shroud. *So be it,* Ali thought.

He searched deep within himself for strength. He was afraid some subliminal command of Fedar's would overpower and stop him, but unlike his attempts to leave the room or use a weapon, this time there was no adverse reaction to his plan. He still had no idea if his scheme would work, and it took every bit of mental energy he possessed to stay connected to himself. He broke out in a sweat, but he hung on and stayed focused. He struggled to maintain his essence even as he felt himself falling into sleep, a slumber that quickly passed into a dream state.

A dream tinged with a ruby-coloured mist…

In the dream, Ali floated out of his body. He could see himself lying on the divan with Fedar still leaning over him. The old man was whispering instructions into his ear.

Fedar said, "You are in my power…"

No, I am not, thought Ali. *I am free.*

He felt a huge weight lift from him. He felt sad too, of course; he'd never wanted to end things like this, but the alternative was to become a puppet and to give Fedar, and his master Savich, control over him and his dreams. And that he could not do.

The old man kept droning on, but Ali paid him little heed. He was watching himself breathing, watching the rise and fall of his chest gradually become slower and slower until it stopped completely.

Fedar suddenly grabbed Ali by the shoulders and shook him. When the boy failed to respond the old man listened vainly for a heartbeat, searched for a pulse, and shook him again.

"*Noooo!*" Fedar cursed, and smashed the beaker against the wall.

That was the last thing Ali saw. Because the next instant he was snatched from the room, out of the physical earthly realm.

8. Flight into Death

Ali found himself floating. No, he was moving, flying, like a cloud scudding across the sky. But, strangely, there was no breeze or wind and he was surrounded by complete emptiness.

Neither dark nor light.

No shades, no shapes.

Nothing…

The only sensation he had was the coppery taste of the dream in his mouth.

He blinked his eyes slowly and looked again. Still the same, *nothing*. It frightened him. This was not death, surely. If not oblivion, Ali had expected something, anything: billowing clouds; the throne of God surrounded by the angels of the Christians and Jews; the idyllic Garden of the Righteous of the Muslims; the heavenly undefiled world of Tengri; crowds of misty wraiths; even hellfire. But *nothing?*

Nothing was impossible to comprehend.

Ever onward he moved, without resistance.

To where…? he wondered.

Time passed but he had no way to measure it. The only thing he had were his thoughts, and they meandered here and charged there with little regard for any form of clock or celestial movement.

Ali thought about the slave girl, Rose. He blamed himself for her capture. If he had only listened to her, been more careful. Even now in death, he felt responsible. He wondered what had become of her, remembering how brave and beautiful she was.

In fact, Ali realised for the first time that he hadn't really stopped thinking about her since the first moment he had seen her on the wharf.

His mind turned to the peculiar sailor and he wondered who *he* was. Ali should have listened to him too, heeded his warning about Fedar. Then he thought about Fedar and wondered how he had been so gullible, how he had allowed himself to fall into the old man's clutches.

Ali did not know who *he* himself was, who his parents were and what had happened to them. Why had he had been cursed with dreams—a legacy from his unknown father—that didn't predict the future, but actually shaped it?

These questions and many others filled his mind as he travelled onward through the void. Until, when he had almost given up to despair, he saw something…

Something small, and far away.

Then it was gone.

But the possibility that something else existed in this place captivated his attention. He strained his eyes hoping to see it again, but he could find no trace of anything. He searched and searched but saw nothing, until he began to wonder if he had imagined it.

Then he saw it again.

Faint and tiny, it was a definite point of light. An unflickering white light so far away it was hardly discernible. He fixed his gaze on it and watched it gradually grow as he approached.

He was so intent on the point of light that he did not feel the temperature dropping. Even when he was so cold that a gnawing numbness made his very essence ache, the vivid brightness of the light still held his full attention.

He was drawn with single-minded purpose towards it, like a moth to a lamp. Larger and larger, brighter and brighter it loomed, until at last he could discern its form, see that it was a massive sphere of pure white light. And it was warm, comfortably warm, like standing in front of a fire on a cold night.

He felt himself slowing until the sense of movement left him completely and he was floating motionless before the immensity of the intense light, like a flea before the sun. His one and only thought was to enter the mighty beacon, to embrace its warmth and defeat the chill spreading through him.

But even as that wish formed in his mind and he felt himself begin to move towards the light again, he was halted abruptly by an overpowering but gentle command:

"No."

His ears and mind were at once filled with it, and he became motionless again.

Before him a dark speck appeared in the core of the radiant sphere, a spot that bloomed little by little until its form became that of a figure, and he realised someone—or something—was approaching him.

Ali was unable to move—for an instant he was filled with foreboding—but the feeling quickly left him, evaporating like the dark come sunrise. It was replaced by a curious warm thrill, a sense of recognition as the figure before him took on the features of a smiling, gentle-faced woman.

Her complexion was pale, her hair so dark against her skin the contrast only made her all the more ghostly, all the more haunting. She was draped in wispy, long-sleeved white robes and there was a translucent quality about her. Some of the light from the sphere passed right through her. Then she spoke, not with her mouth, but in a way that her words formed in his mind.

"My dear boy," she said. Her words brimmed with tenderness, radiating a feeling of love that overwhelmed him. "I am your mother."

"Mother!" Every part of his being screamed the word.

"Please listen to me carefully, for our time is limited. This is wrong. This way is not for you, my son. Your arrival is premature and futile... *Do not* enter the light. As long as you do not enter the light you can go back because up to this point you are still only dreaming."

"But the dreams are my *problem,*" Ali replied. "They cause nothing but trouble."

"You must go back," his mother said. "There is purpose to your life, a reason for your dreams. Merging with the light now is not the answer. You must go back."

"Why me?" Ali asked. "Why do I have these dreams?"

His mother smiled with a touch of sadness. "They belong to you, my son. Welcome them. They are your heritage. Guide them from your heart and mastery will be yours. Trust them, for they will protect you and others. You are destined for bigger things."

Ali shook his head. "I don't understand, they're uncontrollable. They are more like a curse than a blessing."

She nodded. "At first, they are wild, and for you it is even harder because you have no guide, no mentor, but if you follow the way of your heart they will settle. Let them happen, but whatever you do, do not try to consciously force the outcome of your dreams with your thoughts or they will be warped."

She embraced him and her firm hold and warm tears denied the insubstantial look of her. She kissed him on the cheek and her soft lips revived infantile memories of other kisses, tender and loving, denying her death.

"Who am I, mother?" Ali asked.

"Seek Luman," she said. "There you will find answers. Seek Luman and follow your heart. In the meantime, hide your dreams, keep them secret, because Fedar is not the only one who would wish you harm because of what they mean." Again she kissed him, her salty tears trickling down his face. "I love you."

She began to drift away from him back towards the sphere of white light, and he grabbed hold of her sleeve. "What of my father? Did I inherit these dreams from him? Is he with you?"

Suddenly, violently, she was wrenched from his grasp, the fabric of her sleeve parting like cobweb. Ali realised they were both moving, she back into the light and he away from it, both gaining speed ever faster.

Her reply sounded like an echo, distorted and elongated, fading rapidly into inaudibility. "Yourr faatherr isss allivvve, heee issssss…"

Then she was gone.

The white light dwindled rapidly as Ali sped back through the void. Soon the sphere of light was the size of an apple, and before long it was a mere pinprick. Then it disappeared completely.

And with it went the cold, chill ache of death.

Ali woke suddenly, startled, with the disorientating sense of having experienced a particularly vivid and realistic dream. He wondered if he had really crossed over to the other side and met his mother, or if it had all been just a weird dream.

Gradually his surroundings took form. His mouth and nose were filled with a dusty taste and dry smell. He opened his eyes, but it was pitch black and he could see nothing. He became aware of movement, a swaying, bumping motion accompanied by the *clip-clop* of hooves: he was lying on a cart or wagon. And he realised he was quite probably still in danger. Fedar himself might even be driving the vehicle.

His thoughts turned to escape, trying to formulate a way to free himself and get away. Then he nearly cried out in excitement because he realised that he felt none of the illness or restriction Fedar had previously placed on his thoughts. He was free of Fedar's control.

His left arm was lying across his chest, something soft and light balled in his fist. He loosened his grasp and it expanded, filling the cavity his fingers made, downy, fluffy. A small voice in the back of his mind told him not to let go and he squeezed it tight.

He tried to move his right arm, but it was bound, swaddled by some coarse fabric. He tried each of his legs in turn and they encountered the same obstruction. He was swathed in the stuff. He fingered the material, recognising the texture of rough hemp, the very taste that filled his mouth and lungs. He was sealed in a sack.

He inched his right arm across his chest, stretched the hemp, and slid it above his head groping for an opening, but froze instantly at the sound of a voice.

"We gotta be careful getting rid of this body." It was a gravelly voice, unfamiliar to Ali. "Can't just dump him in the Karyağdi, gotta get rid of him good and proper."

"Why?" grunted another voice. "Sounds like a lot of extra work."

"'Cause someone might come looking for him. That's what

Fedar said. That's why he's paying us more than usual."

"So where we taking him?"

A conspiratorial chuckle. "I know a deep hole where no one will ever find him."

They both laughed wickedly, then lapsed back into silence.

Ali knew they were talking about him, about disposing of his body. His *dead* body, or so they thought. Though why he warranted such special treatment was beyond him. Who was there that would come looking for his corpse?

But he was very much alive, not dead. And he had to escape from these miscreants. He continued to grope for an opening, but it was no use: the sack was too tightly bound. He paused to think. Any struggle would reveal he was alive, but to remain where he was meant certain and violent death.

He slid his right hand back stealthily to his waist and was surprised and delighted to find his dagger was still in its scabbard. He drew the blade free, stretched the hemp sacking taut by pushing against it with his feet, and carefully sliced the coarse fabric open. When the slit was long enough, Ali peered through.

Directly overhead, the night sky was sprinkled with glittering stars. Behind and above him sat the dark shapes of the two men driving the wagon.

One of them coughed.

Ali drew the sack closed.

He waited.

When it seemed safe, he lengthened the slit. Soon it reached the point where he could no longer hide his handiwork should one of them look, so he ripped the last section of sacking open with his toes and jerked himself into a sitting position.

From the corner of his eye, Ali saw one of the men turn.

"What the…!" the man exclaimed.

Ali catapulted himself off the back of the wagon. He hit the ground hard, rolling, gravel grazing skin from his left arm and shoulder.

"By God he's alive!" one of the men cried. "Get him."

"Whoa, boy," the other said. "*Whoa*."

Ignoring his pain, Ali glanced furtively from side to side. The dark shape of a man jumped from the still-moving wagon, moonlight glinting coldly from the blade in his hand. Ali turned and plunged into the dense pine woodland alongside the road.

He thrust his way into the forest, branches grabbing at him, scratching and tearing his skin. The men were close behind him, swearing and pushing through the trees. Ali raised his right arm to shield his face and ran even harder, only to smack headlong into the trunk of a large pine tree.

He fell to the ground, his head spinning. He could taste blood and smell leaf mould. He listened for the sounds of pursuit. The men were bellowing and stumbling through the undergrowth nearby, but still out of sight.

He collected himself and shinned one-handed up the very tree he had collided with, his fingers soon sticky with aromatic pine sap. He stopped when he found a perch high on a bough shrouded in its thick needle foliage.

Below him, the two men continued to blunder about the forest. Once they even paused right below him without realising.

"You seen him?" one said.

"Nope," replied the other. "He's vanished. He must be a *jinn*."

"Don't be stupid. We gotta find him. Fedar will skin us alive! You go that way an' I'll go this. We'll meet at the bridge at sunrise."

Ali had no idea where he was, how long he had been bound in the sack or even what direction the men had been travelling, and it was still too dark to try to identify landmarks. Hopefully they were talking about the Karyağdi Bridge, but he could be anywhere so he would have to wait until first light to get his bearings.

The men bashed their way through the undergrowth for hours before they gave up and left. Alone there in the tree with night all around him, Ali realised his left hand was still balled tight, holding something gossamer-like, and his thoughts turned to the encounter with his mother.

She had told him to seek Luman, and that was his intention, but first he wanted to find Rose. It was his fault she had been captured again, and he couldn't stop thinking and worrying about her. There was nothing for it but to set off at first light for İskenderūn, where Fedar said she had been taken.

Besides, İskenderūn was also en-route to Bādiyah Ash-Shām, the vast sand and stone desert, where legend had it Luman dwelt. So, in a way, he was following both pieces of his mother's advice. He was following his heart as well as seeking Luman.

As dawn broke, Ali stretched his limbs, stiff from crouching so long in the pine tree. He winced when he moved his left arm. His shoulder hurt from the fall he took escaping from the men in the cart. It was bruised as well as scraped, but thankfully nothing felt broken.

He looked at his still-clenched fist. After managing to climb the pine tree one-handed, he had clutched it to his heart all night, waiting until he could see what he was desperately holding on to.

When eventually he opened his hand, he realised he was holding a piece of his mother's robe, proving his dream of death had been more than a dream. It was like the stuff of clouds, fluffy, wispy and lustrous. But exposed now to the sunlight, the gossamer fabric dissolved before his eyes, like honey stirred into warm water.

Miraculously, as it evaporated, so too did the pain in his arm and shoulder. His injuries healed in an instant. But Ali was still focused on the last remnant of ethereal stuff in his hand. In moments it was gone completely, yet he still held his empty palm open, staring into it, tears trickling down his cheeks.

9. Escape from Korykos

As luck would have it, Ali was indeed in the forest near the Karyağdi River. He set off to try to cross it, avoiding the Bridge Road itself, travelling instead through the roadside pines, firs and scrubland that climbed towards the Karyağdi Gorge. It was slow, and in some places difficult going, so it took him most of the morning to reach the bridge. He consoled himself, however, with the thought that a small delay was better than being seen by prying eyes.

But crossing the river would be a completely different proposition.

In times past, when the waters of the Karyağdi had been fierce and mighty, they had ripped a great gash across the land. As a result, the now more sedate river lay at the bottom of a deep, impassable gorge. Unless one wanted to travel by the seaward route, which in Ali's case was clearly out of the question because he could not risk going back into town, or by a circuitous north-western route, which would cost weeks and take him many leagues out of his way, the quickest way north-east was to cross the gorge via the Karyağdi Bridge.

But for Ali that was easier said than done, because the hump-backed road that led to the bridge cut its way between two rocky cliff faces that afforded no roadside cover. The moment he stepped onto the road he would be exposed to anyone who might be watching it and anyone travelling along it.

He would be no help to Rose if he was spotted by the wrong people, but any significant delay might also have dreadful consequences for her. He had no choice but to try to cross the bridge. He made his way to the side of the road where he squatted amongst the last few stunted shrubs near the approach to the bridge and watched for guards or travellers.

When it looked clear in both directions, and he could not hear anyone approaching, he broke from cover and dashed towards the bridge. But he was only halfway through the pass, almost to the crest of the road between the cliff faces, when his worst fear came true.

The sound of galloping horses came thudding from behind him.

Dread knotted his stomach and he ran even harder, his heart thumping.

For the moment, the approaching riders were still hidden from him, and he from them, by the forest trees lining the road back the way he had come. But he expected the riders to burst into view at any moment. His only hope was to cross the bridge ahead of them.

But when he reached the crest of the road between the rocky walls, he skidded to a halt.

A fisherman—identifiable by the *nazar* mark painted on his forehead—and a pair of Uzbegs were gathered at the foot of the bridge. To make matters worse, the two mercenaries each had a wolfdog: huge, grey, shaggy, beasts.

Ali wondered in dismay if it might not be better to turn back and face the horsemen after all. The fisherman would recognise him straight away, whereas the riders might not.

But he sensed that danger lay behind as well as ahead. He was trapped with nowhere to turn.

Then he saw an opening, a narrow cleft in the southern cliff face a short way ahead. He lurched towards it. He had no idea if it was deep enough to hide in, but he had no other choice.

He flung himself into the gap half expecting to become wedged in it, but the opening turned out to be deceptively deeper than it looked and he fell flat on his face, grazing his palms and knees on the rocky floor.

He had barely made it.

Moments later he glanced over his shoulder to see three riders astride fast, long-legged Turkoman horses thunder past in a swirl of pounding hooves and dust. He only caught a glimpse of the riders, but he felt certain they too were Uzbegs, the thought of which left him with a queasy, hollow feeling in the pit of his stomach.

Ali crept to the mouth of the crevice, grimacing at the stinging pain of his fresh grazes. If he kept scraping skin off at this rate, he thought with black humour, he would soon have none left.

The horsemen slowed approaching the river, reining their mounts to a halt at the foot of the bridge. They dismounted and the fisherman came forward to greet them. Not only were the riders Uzbegs, but one was the full-bearded, lamellar-and-chainmail-wearing man called Khasis. The one he had glimpsed conspiring with Fedar.

Just then the approaching sound of smaller hooves and crunching gravel could be heard on the road. Ali turned to look. A covered horse carriage was approaching the bridge driven by Fedar's man servant, Sweyn.

Ali jerked back into the shadows, no doubt in his mind as to who the passenger inside the coach was, and gave silent thanks to Luman he had found this hideaway as the carriage rattled past.

After a moment, when it looked as if no one else was following, Ali edged back to his vantage point and looked down at the bridge. Fedar stepped from the carriage and was standing at the foot of the bridge, recognisable by his tall, black-felt *kalpak* hat and long white beard. An icy chill made Ali shiver. Fedar stood with his arms outstretched, magenta cloak spread wide, chanting as the men gathered around him.

Within minutes, hundreds, perhaps thousands of carrion crows arrived at the scene. They preened and fluttered their wings, the afternoon sunlight catching their glossy black plumage. The birds carpeted the bridge and the road, even the sides of the cliff, swarming like vermin. Their tiny yellow eyes and dagger-like beaks all turned towards Fedar.

Abruptly the skull-faced old man let out a piercing screech, a war cry, and flung his arms into the air. The birds rose into the sky in a mighty cloud, casting a shadow over the area so that for a moment it seemed like dusk. The sound of their squawks and beating wings filled the air with a terrible crescendo, then they scattered to all points of the compass.

Ali retreated back into the depths of the crevice and crumpled to the ground. The situation felt hopeless, but when he thought of Rose, of her plight, he knew he had to find a way to go on. The best thing would be to wait for night to give himself the greatest chance of success.

When it was full dark, Ali stretched his cramped and sore muscles. He massaged his calves and rolled his neck. He had been waiting for hours and was impatient to leave the confinement of his hiding place. Fedar and his henchmen had packed and left shortly after the scene he had witnessed, some going north-east and the others returning to Korykos. He hoped the birds were roosting for the night, but he guessed there would still be men guarding the bridge.

He stole along the road approaching the bridge, hugging the cliff face. At the foot of the bridge, he paused in a shadow and listened.

Nothing…

He moved onto the bridge and a cry rang out.

"Hey you!"

He turned to see a tall, skinny fisherman charging towards him like a raging bull. Ali held his ground, his gaze locked on the man. At the last moment, when the attacker leaped at him, Ali crouched down, only to spring back to his feet as the fisherman tumbled over him. Ali's manoeuvre, and the man's own momentum, catapulted the sentry over the side of the bridge.

The fisherman's cry rang out in the night as he fell into the darkness.

Then it stopped abruptly and Ali prayed the man had hit the water rather than the rocks at the bottom of the gorge. He glanced swiftly around. The pair of Uzbegs and their hounds appeared to have gone. Ali stole across the bridge. When he reached the other side, and it was obvious nobody else was following, he paused and turned momentarily back towards Korykos.

In the distance, pinpoints of light shone from the lamps of outlying farm cottages. Otherwise, the city gave the impression it was asleep. Despite that, Ali knew the tavernas would be alive with laughter and music, the night markets filled with the babble of voices and the aroma of roasting meat dripping sizzling hot fat onto charcoal fires.

Ali wondered if he would ever return to the city. The trouble with the Korykos fishermen was one thing, and might in time blow over, but his focus now was on finding and rescuing Rose, on the mystery of Luman, and finding a way to either tame or rid himself of these weird dreams. After that, if he survived, who knew? Perhaps he would return, but he thought not. He had always believed his destiny lay beyond living on the streets of Korykos, that he was meant for other things, things that would help make both his life and the world a better place.

He certainly did not want to see the scheming, two-faced Fedar ever again, unless it was to extract some sort of justice or retribution. Scary as it felt, it was time to start a new life, perhaps with Rose if all went well. With a small sigh and a pang of something like regret, but not quite, he turned his back on the city that had been his home for as long as he could remember, and set off at a run into the dark, along the road north-east, leaving Korykos behind.

He ran until a stitch cramped his side and he had to slow to relieve it. Then he decided to continue at walking pace and keep to the side of the road. It was safer. That way he could listen for any traffic and move into the underbrush when necessary, before anyone knew he was there.

Half a dozen times during the night he heard people approaching from one direction or the other and he hid from view until they had passed. There was a farmer bringing a cartload of produce to town. A few message riders galloping between towns. And a group of drunken farm labourers stumbling home singing bawdy ditties at the top of their voices.

Then, just when he thought he was safe, the chilling howl of a wolfdog ripped through the night.

Ali's blood ran cold.

The call of the dog was followed by a shout and the sound of running feet ahead.

Ali scrambled down the shrubby bank beside the road and burrowed under a thicket in the dark gully at the bottom.

A wolfdog snarled and growled; this time much closer.

Then a pair of the slavering animals reached the spot where Ali had left the road, barking in unison. A man shouted a command and the wolfdogs fell silent.

Ali held his breath, trembling in terror. He could smell the wet-blanket odour of the half-wild animals, hear them snuffling for his scent.

"Probably another fox," an Uzbeg voice said.

"Let the wolfdogs loose," another man said.

"Took us half an hour to get 'em back last time," the Uzbeg said.

"Khasis said to take no chances," the second replied.

One of the wolfdogs let out a low, rumbling growl.

Further back along the road there was a noise in the underbrush, and the wolfdogs barked and howled again. Branches cracked and broke as something hurried away from the beasts.

"Come on," said the Uzbeg. "Over there."

"We should search here," the second man said.

"Whatever was here is now over there. Come on."

The men and the dogs took off back along the way Ali had come, the wolfdogs snuffling and howling at some new quarry.

Ali let out a long, slow breath and waited for his pulse to slow.

When the hunters were far enough away, he quietly made his way north-east again. Behind him the two men and their half-wild, bark-howling scent hounds crashed through the undergrowth, chasing a rabbit, stoat, or some other hapless animal.

After a while Ali re-joined the road, walking quickly, but quietly, to put as much distance between him and the night hunters as possible. He pressed on until the grey half-light of dawn showed on the eastern horizon, and birds began to twitter and chirp in their nests and roosts. He knew then he had to find a place to hide before the black carrion crows were up and about.

He spotted a haystack in a field beside the road and burrowed inside where he curled up, exhausted from his night's escapade.

As he drifted off to sleep, the idea struck him that perhaps he could use his dreams to help Rose, direct their power to free her. Fedar had said that he could control his dreams and create the future. His mother, on the other hand, had warned him not to consciously try to control his dreams, but she had also said that he could direct them from his heart.

He fell asleep with images of Rose in his mind. And he did indeed dream of the slave girl, but it was not a red-tinged prophetic dream, rather a nightmare that detailed her captivity and torments, and left him feeling helpless and guilty.

10. Carrion Crows

It was late afternoon, almost sunset when Ali woke and peered out from his hiding spot under the haystack. The low sun cast long shadows across the land. On the western horizon the clouds were tinged coral pink.

But the pleasure of the scene was short lived, because perched in the trees along the roadside were the unmistakable dark shapes of watching crows. Like sentinels, they were positioned at regular intervals, their heads turning this way and that, observing both the road and the surrounding countryside.

They were watching for him.

Across the road, a murder of crows was swarming through a grove of mature fig trees, squawking and fighting, feasting on the ripe, purple-brown fruit.

After a while, rain started to fall. Not in steady droplets the way it usually did this time of year, but in a torrential downpour that felt warm when Ali reached his cupped palm out to catch some of the water to wet his mouth. The air was thick with the odour of petrichor. The rain kept falling through twilight and dusk. The only good thing about it was that it drove the crows under cover, but Ali knew they would still be watching.

When it was dark, he ventured from under the haystack and was drenched in a matter of moments. There was nothing for it but to press on, because the rain was relentless and would likely continue all night.

He trudged along the road, the drumming rain so loud it drowned out the sound of his footsteps. That was a good thing, he decided, that and the fact the rain would keep most other travellers off the road. But he did not realise how loud it actually was until there was an *araba,* a box-covered horse cart, suddenly beside him, its wheels throwing up splashes of mud.

Ali cursed his stupidity and lowered his head, hoping the driver would ignore him. But the wagon pulled to a halt a short way ahead and a figure leaned out and hailed him.

Ali almost fled, but then he realised what the stranger was saying.

"Do you want a ride? It's dry up here."

Why not? Ali thought. The man had already seen him and he didn't look like one of Fedar's henchmen. Ali took hold of his proffered hand and climbed beside him on the driver's seat.

"Thank you," he said, raising his eyes to indicate the canopy above them. "It's better to ride under cover than walk in this weather."

"Better than walking in any weather," the driver replied, chuckling. "Besides, I enjoy the company. There's not too many people travel by night. Gee-up," he said to the horse, and the wagon lurched into motion. "My name's Jemal. I'm going through to İskenderūn, if that's any help."

"Thank you," Ali said, not mentioning his own name. He regarded Jemal speculatively.

"The only thing is," the driver went on, "we have to travel by night and rest by day." He gave another friendly chuckle. "Hope you don't mind."

It was too good to be true. It was perfect. Ali wondered if he had unwittingly fallen into the clutches of one of Fedar's cronies after all, someone who knew his plight and was playing on it. But the man's genial manner felt genuine.

"I don't mind at all, I'm grateful for the ride."

"It's because of my cargo," the man added. "Sluglows. I bring 'em all the way from a small island in the Sea of Murmans. It's a long way when you only travel by night."

"I don't understand," Ali said, frowning. "Why do you only travel at night?"

"The sluglows are too heavy to haul overland by day," he said.

"I can bring twenty times as many when I avoid the daylight."

"Slug what?"

"Slu-*glows*. You know, float-lanterns, those little bugs that float into the air and glow like lanterns when the sun goes down, then turn dull and grey and drop to the ground like a lump of lead when the sun rises."

He chuckled again. It was a friendly, warm sound. "I reckon they weigh the same as lead during the day too because they're too heavy to haul. But by night they're light as air. One horse can pull a wagonful. And in İskenderūn I can get a good price, the rich folk there prize these little creatures."

The horse was certainly setting a good pace despite the wagon it was hauling. After a while the rain stopped and a breeze sprang up, carrying with it a rich, earthy scent. The wind cut through his wet clothes, and Ali shivered and hugged his arms around himself.

Jemal noticed and pointed under the seat. "There's a spare cloak there you can have if you're cold. Somebody left it behind once. It's too small for me, but it was too good to throw away so I kept it."

The cloak, complete with cowl, was woven from good quality, though worn, dark-green wool. As good if not better than a blanket. Ali said thanks and wrapped it gratefully around himself while the driver continued to prattle on.

In fact, Jemal kept up a virtual monologue for most of the night, entertaining Ali with tales of his wanderings and philandering. The man hardly noticed whether Ali was listening or not, oblivious to those times when his attention strayed. Those moments when Ali thought he could hear malevolent sounds in the night sky, distant calls, fluttering. Other times when he felt like they were being watched. Jemal continued to talk and joke, chuckling merrily, completely unaware of Ali's unease.

Shortly before dawn, Jemal turned to him and said, "Are you sleepy, boy? There's a fishing village ahead called Akyatan. We'll be welcome there and fed and provided with a place to bed down free of charge. On my last trip I presented a sluglow to the village elder and he reciprocated with a standing invitation to stay whenever I'm passing through."

They crested a small hill and looked down on the village. In the faint moonlight Ali could make out a ramshackle collection of buildings and huts set on stilts in the water of a broad, flat lagoon.

"That's the Akyatan Gölü," Jemal said, licking his lips. "Best seafood to be had for leagues. Grey mullet, bream, sea bass, eels, and blue crabs. We'll eat like sultans here, lad."

The huts over the water were connected to each other, and to the buildings on the mainland, by a series of rickety wooden catwalks. There were dark shapes that looked like canoes or boats moored beneath them.

Jemal pulled the wagon into a cutting at the side of the road above the village and jumped down to tend the horse.

"Can I have a peek at the sluglows?" Ali asked, climbing to the ground from the driver's passenger seat.

"Sure, but I can only open the back a crack because I don't want them to escape."

Jemal led the way to the rear of the wagon where he unlocked the iron clasp holding the door shut and opened it a finger's width. Light shone out, startling Ali. He put an eye to the gap, blinking as his vision adjusted to the brightness, and gasped in wonder. Hundreds of egg-shaped creatures floated like jellyfish in the sea, swirling and billowing, each glowing like white-hot coals in the heart of a blazing fire.

"Wow!" Ali said.

Jemal shut the rear door and fastened the clasp. Then he set the horse free to graze with some other animals nearby. Lastly, he cupped his hands to his mouth and made a loud, shrill screech. From the wagon there came a *thump* and it swayed, its timbers groaning as it settled.

Jemal laughed. "Another thing that makes these sluglows fall is a swamp-owl cry. There's not a spark amongst them now."

Ali shook his head in amazement.

"You can try it next time. After hearing a cry like that they'll stay down and out long enough for the sun to rise. It would take a team of horses to steal this wagon now." Jemal laughed again. It was infectious, and soon Ali was laughing too.

They sat on a grassy verge until the first light of dawn had broken over the Amanus Mountains, across the Gulf of İskenderūn, and there were signs of activity in the village. For much of the night's journey, Ali had managed to push the feeling of impending doom to the back of his mind. But as he got to his feet, birds were chirping in the nearby trees, and the dread of being caught reasserted itself. He tugged the cowl of his newly acquired cloak low over his face and hurried to follow Jemal down a winding dirt path to the village.

Before they retired to get some sleep, Ali and Jemal ate a large bowl of delicious *balık buğulama,* the local spicy fish stew, in the village kitchen. When they had mopped the last of the gravy up with pieces of salty, unleavened bread, they were guided along a catwalk over the lagoon to a small single-room hut on stilts, where seagrass mats had been laid out on the floor for them.

Ali went to the window and leaned out to close the storm shutters, as much because of the uncomfortable feeling he was being watched as to keep the light out. But despite his fear, he paused a moment to peer out across the mirror-flat water and admire the simple, idyllic beauty of the place. One could fish from the bedroom window or step out the door and dive into the water for a refreshing swim in the lagoon.

It was a kind of paradise, he thought, yawning as he pulled the shutters closed.

He was exhausted, but when he stretched out on the seagrass mat and closed his eyes, sleep eluded him. A creeping unease infected his mood. The same sense of dread he had felt before Jemal had picked him up. To deflect the feeling, he thought about trying to use his dreams to aid his quest.

His mother had told him not to consciously try to control his dreams, warning him that if he did the results would be corrupted. Instinctively, he knew that to be true. But she had also told him to trust them, to guide them from his heart. So that was what he tried to do, focusing his thoughts on Rose and her plight. Despite that, his attempt to dream about her came to nothing. Instead he slept fitfully and had unsettling dreams about wolfdogs and carrion crows.

Ali woke in the late afternoon, roused by Jemal's own waking movements. A sense of unease, of anxiety and dread, lingered briefly after his nightmarish dreams. But these feelings were dispelled when he came fully awake and the rank stench hit him. It assailed his nostrils no matter which way he turned, permeating the room, putrid and decaying.

Even worse, the screeches and caws of crows came from close by outside.

Jemal rose from his bed, went to the window, and reached for the shutters.

Ali lurched to his feet. "Don't open the shutters!"

"Morning, boy." Jemal let out his familiar chuckle. "I hope this stink won't put you off your breakfast."

"Wait 'til it's dark," Ali insisted. "The crows are out there. I can hear them."

Jemal frowned at Ali, puzzled, and threw the shutters aside anyway. "Crows? They can't hurt you."

Ali peered out. The water surrounding the huts had vanished. The tide had gone out while they were sleeping, leaving in its wake a sea of putrid, slimy black mud. Paradise indeed. His eyes narrowed and he held his mouth tight. Moving across the mudflats were scores of black crows. He felt his chest tighten and had to force himself to breathe.

"Close the shutters!" Ali hissed. "Those birds are evil."

As if to corroborate his claim, half a dozen or more of the black birds set upon a hapless gull that was scavenging alongside them. When they dispersed, all that remained of the gull were some blood-stained white feathers pressed into the mud.

Then there was a flutter of wings and one of the crows landed on the window sill. It peered past them into the room, bobbing and weaving its head, searching for titbits. Then it saw Ali and froze, a low sound rumbling in its throat.

Unaware of the change in the bird's attitude, Jemal reached out his finger to pet it.

The bird launched itself at him in a flurry of wings. Its claws found his face and gouged long furrows down his cheek.

Jemal wailed and ripped the thing off him.

Ali ducked and scuttled, bent over, to the window. He slammed the shutters closed and straightened to face his companion. The bird lay limply in Jemal's hands, its neck wrung. Jemal stood looking at Ali, his mouth opening and closing like he wanted to say something but could not remember the words.

"I told you not to open the shutters." Ali's eyes were wide, his body tense. "I heard them out there. They're here for me."

Jemal glanced distastefully at the dead bird and dropped it. "Now I understand your concern about them," he said, dabbing at the wounds on his face. "But they haven't come here for you, boy. They're always here. The villagers throw their scraps, fish heads, guts and the like into the water. When the tide goes out the birds come to scavenge for what's left behind."

It seemed like a reasonable explanation, but Ali knew better.

11. The Thief

Four nights later, just before dawn, they were coming to the end of their journey, approaching İskenderūn along the coast road. The only sounds were the *clip-clop* of the horse's tread on the hard-packed road and the gentle *swish* of waves breaking on the seashore to their right.

"See that?" Jemal said, pointing to a jagged tower of hewn stones. It was little more than a dark shape looming beside the road in the half-light. "That's the Tower of Jonah. Where the prophet was disgorged by the whale that swallowed him."

"There are no whales in the Mediterranean," Ali said.

"According to the scriptures there was one. That's faith."

Ali gave a disdainful snort.

"What's wrong?" Jemal asked. "Don't you believe in God?"

"Oh, I believe in God," Ali said. "I just don't believe in religion. The Jews, Muslims and Christians all supposedly believe in the same god, but they argue their differences and persecute and fight wars against each other all in the name of God."

Jemal was silent for a moment. Then he sighed. "Sadly, that's true."

Half an hour later, they passed beneath the massive sandstone arch between the two towers of the north gate into the city of İskenderūn. A pair of nightwatchmen huddled over a dull brazier at the entrance to the city all but ignored their passing.

Birds were chirping and tweeting their morning song in the trees, and a müezzin's call rang out from the minaret of a nearby mosque. A rooster crowed in the distance.

Jemal pulled the horse to a halt at a travellers' inn inside the gate and said, "This is where we stop, boy. The sluglows'll be droppin' any time soon."

Ali jumped down from the wagon and stretched. He sniffed the air. The city stank of ordure and wood smoke.

Jemal joined him and yawned. "Are you sure you don't want to stay here a bit and grab something to eat and have a bit of a nap?"

Ali gave him a resolute smile and shook his head.

"I know, I know, you told me. You've got an urgent matter to attend to." Jemal took Ali by the hand. "Goodbye and good luck, boy." For once he did not laugh.

Ali bid Jemal farewell and strode into the unfamiliar city. İskenderūn was the original port on the narrow plain between the Mediterranean Sea and the Amanus Mountains—founded by Alexander the Great after he defeated the Persians—larger and older, more congested and seedier than Korykos. The rich people here were richer and the poor folk poorer.

Even at this early hour touts tugged at his arm, cajoling him to follow them to cheap lodgings. Beggars plied their trade, mistaking Ali for a person of means. Hucksters offered him amulets and souvenirs, and food cart vendors tried to entice him with their trays of warm *simit*, bread rings encrusted with sesame seeds and crisp-fried anchovies, sticky with grape molasses.

His stomach rumbled and growled but he kept on with single-minded purpose. Jemal's company had been distracting and comforting, but now that he was here in İskenderūn he couldn't waste any time. He was headed for the docks to find information about the slave ship. To find out what had happened to Rose.

The waterfront was already abuzz by the time he arrived. Foreigners and locals alike hurried along the quayside. Ribald voices, squeals of debauchery and sea chants spilled from the tavernas. The raised voices of hucksters spruiking for trade and the odour of frying fish filled the air.

Here Ali felt less conspicuous. People on the waterfront rubbed shoulders with strangers every day. To them he was just another face in the crowd, a new arrival looking for an inn. But not just *any* inn. Ali was looking for a *suitable* inn. One that was patronised by locals rather than visitors, avoided by the harlots and cutpurses.

He was walking along a narrow, cobbled alley when suddenly a skinny, black-haired boy in a red vest and butter-yellow *şalvar* pants brushed past him running full pelt. Hard on his heels, two young men wearing identical raw cotton baggy pants and loose shirts, were gaining on him.

"*Hirsiz!*" one of them yelled. It was a word Ali knew well. *Thief.*

They shoved Ali aside, and the one in the lead launched himself at the running boy, tackling him to the stony cobbles. The boy writhed and squirmed trying to break free of his captor, but the second man—a huge fellow with big, broad shoulders and arms as thick as tree limbs—joined the fray and pummelled the boy with fists the size of ham hocks.

The first man, the one who had tackled the boy to the ground, climbed to his knees and drew a dagger.

"Stop!" Ali cried as the man raised the weapon to strike.

Ali looked left and right, scooped up a piece of broken cobble, and flung it as hard as he could at the dagger-wielding man.

It struck him in the head with a loud *smack*. The man cried out in pain and dropped the weapon, blood trickling down his forehead.

His accomplice roared in anger and turned on Ali, swinging a wild round-house fist at his face. Ali ducked, none too soon, feeling the air from the mistimed blow ruffle his long hair.

Ali kicked him in the groin as hard as he could; the big man let out a loud *oomph* and his knees buckled.

Just then a third man, older than the pair who had chased and attacked the boy, but dressed exactly the same as them, approached the fray, gasping. His arrival gave the other two pause.

"Why are you doing this?" Ali said to the attackers. "You'll kill him."

"He's a thief," said the big man, still bent over breathing deeply, hands on his knees to steady himself.

"What did he steal?" asked Ali.

"Bread," the old man replied, catching his breath. "We are bakers and he stole bread from us."

Ali turned to face the old man, noting his long grey beard, his face creased and wrinkled as a prune, an embroidered white skullcap on his head.

"Hajji," Ali said, honouring the old man with the recognition that he had made the Muslim pilgrimage to Mecca. "Look at this skinny boy. He must be starving."

The three men gazed at the boy on the ground, who was now stirring.

"Hey, boy," Ali said. "Why did you steal bread from these good bakers? Are you hungry?"

The boy lifted his head and nodded. Ali was shocked to see that he had only one eye, a livid pink scar running down the left-hand side of his face from his forehead through the empty socket to his cheek.

"Good bakers," Ali said, meeting the older man's gaze, "your holy book asks you to feed the hungry, yet you were going to cut, maybe kill him."

The men exchanged glances with each other.

"He is a Greek *gâvur*," the baker with the dagger said, gingerly touching his forehead where Ali's stone had hit him.

"So what?" Ali said, "All sorts of people live here: Turks, Armenians, Mamluks, Bulgarians, Kazakhs, you name it. He is a person. Not only is he hungry, but he only has one eye." Ali pulled out his calfskin purse. "Shame on you. How much was the bread? I will pay you for it."

The man with the dagger hawked and spat. "We are not wealthy," he said. "Stealing our bread is like taking food from the mouths of our family. And he has stolen from us other times."

The old man looked at his feet, embarrassed. "If the one-eyed boy promises not to steal from us again, my sons and I will forgive him this time. And there is no need for you to pay for the bread he stole."

"But this time only," the big one said, his face still flushed with anger.

Ali helped the boy up from the ground. The piece of purloined bread now lay broken and mashed on the cobbles.

"Come on," Ali said. "Let's get out of here before they change their minds."

12. A New Friend

The one-eyed boy in the red vest led Ali to a taverna called the Lemon Tree. Inside, it was filled with the murmur of conversation and the rattle of dice, and smelled strongly of sour, fermented *boza,* the local milky beer-like drink. Ali made his way to the bar, purchased them each a slice of *manakish*—flatbread topped with spiced ground beef—and a clay cup of hot mint tea sweetened with honey. They found seats on a bench at the rear of the common room from where they could observe the other patrons.

Ali sipped his tea, enjoying its clean, fresh flavour. The other customers were a mixed bunch: boatmen, stevedores, a few merchants, and even a Dervish *fakir* sitting alone clicking prayer beads softly through his fingers. For the most part the people drank and chatted and laughed among themselves, paying neither Ali nor his new friend any heed.

"I am indebted to you," the one-eyed boy said, gulping down his *manakish*. "Not only did you save my life, but now you're feeding me, a thief."

Ali smiled. "I know what it's like to be hungry."

"What brings you here to this city?"

"I'm looking for someone," Ali said, chewing as he spoke, savouring the sweet herbal earthiness of the onion and thyme used to spice the *manakish*.

"Someone from Korykos perhaps?" The boy gave him a wink, inclining his head with exaggeration so that he didn't just look like he was blinking his one eye.

Ali considered him with suspicion.

"I might only have one eye," the stranger said, "but I don't miss much. My ears see too." He grinned knowingly at Ali's wary expression. "It's your accent, the way you form your words. The Korykos way."

Ali decided that he was in no real danger from this fellow, perhaps even in a position to gain some information. The boy looked to be about his own age, probably fifteen or sixteen, though somewhat taller than himself.

"Your accent doesn't sound like you're from here either," Ali said.

"My name is Demetri," the one-eyed boy said with a friendly, lopsided grin. His good eye was dark brown, bright and alert. "You're right, I'm not from here. But I've been living here for almost a year and I know most of the comings and goings around Alexandretta. If you tell me who it is you're looking for I might be able to help."

"İskenderūn, you mean," Ali said, not offering his own name.

Demetri laughed. "I'm Greek. In my family we call the city by its original name, after Alexander the Great."

Ali shrugged. "I'm searching for a friend who was aboard a sleek foreign galley decorated with pennants and fancy carvings. It probably docked here about three or four days ago."

"So," Demetri said, knowingly, "your friend is a slave."

Ali's eyes went wide.

"If your friend was aboard the ship you've described, then they are either a slave or a slaver. That boat is a galley from the Maghreb, out of Tunis, carrying poor wretches bound for the auction block. And by the looks of you, I doubt your friend is a slaver."

"You've seen it?" Ali asked, his expression earnest. "When? Where is it?"

Demetri looked him up and down appraisingly. "What's it worth to you?"

Just then, two Uzbegs in mercenary garb staggered drunkenly in through the doorway. The conversation in the inn stopped and the Uzbegs stood there, swaying slightly, surveying the surroundings with bleary eyes. Ali pulled the cowl of his cloak lower over his face and shuffled aside to block their view of him.

"Come on," one of the mercenaries slurred. "No fun 'ere, let's go."

The door slammed shut behind them and the buzz of normal conversation returned to the inn.

Demetri was watching Ali sharply, reappraising him. "You hid yourself from those men," he said without accusation.

Ali felt himself blush. "No, I ah…"

Demetri was nodding his head in a knowing manner.

"You asked what it was worth to me to know about the slave galley," Ali said, changing the subject and returning to their previous conversation. "It's worth a great deal. But as for payment, I'm afraid I have nothing much of value to offer you apart from my friendship and gratitude."

Surprisingly, Demetri laughed and said, "Fair enough. I thought as much. Besides, it's me who owes you gratitude." He leaned closer and lowered his voice. "The galley you mentioned is moored at the quay, but that no longer matters because the slaves have already been moved to a holding pen in readiness for the auction later this morning."

"This morning!" It came out louder than Ali intended.

A few heads turned their way.

Demetri put a finger to his lips. "Since Sultan Bayezid's death the empire has collapsed into chaos, and the slave trade has fallen into the hands of local Beys and pirates. Here the Mamluks rule, but their Sultan is a long way away in Cairo. So the pirates hold private auctions and pay no taxes. But don't worry, I know where it is being held."

"Then let's go," Ali said, standing. "Take me there."

They left the inn and made their way through the quayside fish market, past stalls of silvery mullet, blue whiting and slippery eels, tables spread with clams and mussels, and red-faced women plucking orange-red crabs from cauldrons of steaming water.

Moving away from the docklands, Demetri led Ali east through the laundry district, along a lane bordered on one side with rows and rows of lines hung with wet washing. The whole area was a sea of sheets, towels and clothing of all shapes and colours gently flapping in the breeze.

Suddenly, Demetri shoved Ali into a line of washing. "Hide," he said under his breath.

Ali staggered through two or three rows of damp fabric until he came to a halt, tangled in a large cotton sheet.

"Hey you," called a gruff voice with the Tajiki Persian accent of an Uzbeg.

Ali's heart missed a beat and he froze.

"Me?" Demetri said innocently.

"Yes, you," the speaker said. "Who was that with you?"

"Just a washer-girl," Demetri said.

"Trying to have a feel, were you?" the speaker said, sniggering.

"Never mind that," said another Tajiki-accented voice. "Look at this sketch. Have you seen this boy?"

Ali peeped between the rows of damp laundry and saw the two Uzbegs, one of them thrusting a piece of paper at Demetri.

"We're looking for him. His name's Ali. There's a handsome reward for information."

Ali held his breath, his hands trembling.

Demetri studied the drawing. After a moment he shook his head.

Ali relaxed a little.

"What's he done?" Demetri asked.

"Never you mind," the Uzbeg with the paper said. "Just keep your eyes open. We'll make it worth your while if you help us find him."

"Where's your girl?" the other Uzbeg said, peering into the sea of damp fabric. "Perhaps she's seen him."

Ali shrank back into the flapping laundry.

"Gone." Demetri raised his hands in a *who knows* gesture. "We had an argument."

"Said *no*, did she?" He gave a nasty laugh.

"Let's keep moving," the other said, and they strode along the lane and halted at one of the laundry doors before going inside.

"Come on," Demetri called in a low, urgent voice.

Ali emerged from his hiding place and they hurried along the lane away from the Uzbegs.

"Where did *they* come from?" Ali asked.

Demetri glanced back. "I saw them come out of one of the laundries."

"You could have sold me out," Ali said.

Demetri halted and turned to face him. "Aside from the fact I am indebted to you, I like you. And I don't like them. I saw your reaction to the Uzbegs in the Lemon Tree and figured you didn't want to be seen by them. It's as simple as that."

Ali reached out and laid a hand on his arm. "The picture, was it...?"

"You?" Demetri inclined his head in acknowledgement. "Yes, it was you, Ali. I assume that's your name. Quite a good likeness, actually."

"Shit!" Ali pulled his cowl lower over his eyes. "I'm surprised you weren't tempted by the reward."

"Those Uzbegs mercenaries are barbarians." Demetri hawked and spat on the ground with loathing. "They raid innocent villages and farms. They rob local traders and rape womenfolk. And if that's not enough, how do you think I lost my eye?"

Ali considered the one-eyed boy's face. "They did that to you?"

Demetri nodded bitterly, his face contorted with grief and fury. "That's why I intend to go back to Greece. After Timur Lenk defeated the Christian Knights Hospitaller at Smyrna, he ordered his men to destroy the fortifications and massacre the population."

Ali grimaced. He had heard the stories.

"They beheaded hundreds of people and mounted their severed heads on stakes. Then his horde travelled back east, full of blood lust. They razed our village. With my own eyes I saw his Uzbegs murder my mother and father, and when I tried to help, they left me for dead with this"—he pointed to his missing eye—"as a reminder of what they had done."

"Then you'll be pleased to know," Ali said, "that by helping me you'll be working against them."

"Why are they after you?" Demetri asked.

"They're employed by evil men who want something I have," Ali said.

Demetri took a step back. "I thought you were poor. You told me you had nothing of value to offer me."

Ali closed his eyes and gave a small shake of his head. "It's not money or a physical thing they're after. It's something in my head. I don't know why I've got it and I don't want it."

"Something you know?"

"It's not that simple, and you wouldn't believe me if I told you. Besides, it's safer for both of us if you don't know. If it makes you feel any better, these Uzbegs don't know either. They're just doing what they're told. Working for the men who pay their wages."

"Makes sense," Demetri said. "Since the collapse of Timur Lenk's army, the nomad Uzbeg and Jagatai mercenaries are happy to sell their swords to the highest bidder. The bloodier the work, the better. They enjoy it."

Ali glanced nervously behind. A peculiar sense that he was being watched made the tiny hairs on the back of his neck prickle and stand on end. "Let's keep moving, I don't feel comfortable here."

"It's not far now," Demetri said, taking off at a trot.

Ali kept pace with him but the feeling of being watched did not go away. He kept glancing back over his shoulder, half expecting to see Fedar or Khasis with some of his Uzbegs creeping up behind them.

But the lane appeared empty.

Then he looked up…

There were carrion crows perched on the rooftops and chimneys, silhouetted against the sky. Dark shapes watching and waiting.

His stomach went tight and his heart squeezed painfully in his chest. He tried to swallow, but his mouth was dry. "Hurry," he said. "We have to hurry."

13. The Slave Market

"That's the slave market," Demetri said, pointing.

Ali looked and his heart fell.

A pair of enormous, bare-chested and shaven-headed brutes armed with short, curved swords stood guard before an ironclad gate set in a high sandstone wall surrounding some sort of compound.

"We'll never get past those guards," Ali said.

But Demetri was unfazed and led Ali instead to a dirt alley that ran alongside the perimeter wall of the compound. Partway along it the one-eyed boy stopped where the high wall was covered with a tangle of gnarled old grapevines. They had been recently picked clean of ripe fruit; all that remained were a few shrivelled brown bunches still hanging in places, rotting on the vine.

"We can observe the goings-on from up there," Demetri said.

As if on cue, the deep beat of a drum resonated from the other side of the wall—*boom, boom, boom*—heralding the beginning of proceedings.

Demetri scaled the wall by using the branches of the twisted grapevines like a ladder. Ali paused to scan the vines, the wall and the surrounding buildings for crows, then followed him when he was satisfied the area was clear. At the top they peered down into the compound below.

In the centre of the courtyard a lanky, dark-skinned drummer stood on a raised wooden platform, stolidly beating a large double-sided *davul* with wooden mallets. The drum was supported by a rope around the back of his neck and hung sideways in front of him, so he could beat one side with his left hand and the other with his right.

In front of the drummer, a puffy, round-faced man in white robes was leaning on a stout wooden staff and smiling down at the people gathered in a half-circle around the improvised podium.

"How is it this friend of yours is a slave?" Demetri asked. "How do you know him?"

"*Her,*" Ali said. "My friend is a her, not a him. Her name is Rose."

"Ahhh, I *see.*" Demetri gave Ali a knowing one-eyed wink. "It's like that, is it?"

Ali's face flushed. "No, it's not 'like that'."

Demetri chuckled and poked Ali in the ribs. "Sure. That's why you're going to so much trouble to help her."

"I'm helping her because it's my fault she was captured," Ali said.

Demetri grunted and looked away, a little abashed.

Ali surveyed the scene. Guards, armed with long-handled *tabar* axes with large, crescent-shaped blades, were stationed at strategic points around the courtyard, watching the proceedings with a wary eye.

"I have to find a way to get in there," he said.

"And do what?" Demetri asked.

"Rescue Rose, of course."

"You wouldn't stand a chance."

"I'll find a way," Ali said, his eyes cold and determined.

Demetri smacked his forehead with the palm of his hand. "To get yourself killed! Don't be stupid. We can watch from up here, find out who buys her and follow them when they leave."

The drummer stopped and the portly, round-faced man flourished his staff and struck the base of it three times on the platform decking.

Conversation amongst the crowd ceased.

"Lot number one…" he announced.

Ali bit his lip and leaned forward.

A guard swung open the heavy timber door of a large sandstone blockhouse in the corner of the courtyard and another guard bustled a stocky, muscular man—his wrists and ankles shackled, his head hung in submission—out across the yard and up the steps onto the platform.

"A solid workhorse," the auctioneer called, poking the slave with his staff. "Now good people, what am I bid?"

The auction had begun.

Ali felt sick to his stomach.

At first the bidding for the man on the block was brisk, people making bids with signals undetectable to the untrained eye. Then the bidders gradually dropped off until there was only one left.

"Five gold ducats going once," the auctioneer bellowed, thumping his staff on the wooden floor of the platform. "Five gold ducats going twice..." He paused with his staff raised, ready to strike again. "Last chance, do I hear five and a half...?"

And so it went on. The proceedings continued throughout the day in a similar manner. Men, women and children of all races, shapes and sizes were put up for auction.

For some—those with attributes in demand: skilled tradesmen, virgin girls and the healthy young—the bidding was brisk. But in the end even the other poor souls for whom the bidding was less enthusiastic were sold with the aid of the auctioneer's skilful patter.

With each new lot, with each opening of the heavy timber door, Ali leaned forward and held his breath in anticipation. Only to slump with despair each time when Rose failed to appear.

Sixty-seven lots in all and there was no sign of Rose whatsoever.

"Where is she?" Ali said wretchedly.

"Perhaps she's already escaped," Demetri said.

"We've got to find out what's happened to her."

Down in the courtyard a white-robed and turbaned gatekeeper swung open the iron-clad perimeter gate and people began to leave.

"See that gatekeeper there?" Demetri said.

Ali looked to where he was pointing.

"I know him, his name is Abdullah. I met him in the bazaar when I first arrived in town. Maybe he can tell us what has happened to your friend Rose. Tell me what she looks like and

I'll go down and ask him."

"I'm coming with you," Ali insisted.

Demetri shook his head. "It's too risky. That sketch the Uzbegs showed me looked a lot like you."

"I'll pull my hood low over my face," Ali said.

"You'll be no help to her if you get captured."

Ali's shoulders wilted. He knew Demetri was right, but he hated feeling so helpless. He gave him a description of Rose and grudgingly watched his newfound friend descend the grapevine and run along the alleyway and around the corner.

Moments later Demetri stepped into the entrance of the compound and beckoned the gatekeeper. The white-clad man named Abdullah sauntered over to him and the pair had a brief conversation which concluded with a handshake. Demetri then slipped back out the gate and before long he was back again.

"What did you find out?" Ali asked.

Demetri grimaced. "She's been sold."

"But we watched the entire auction," Ali said, puzzled.

"Apparently she was never part of the auction consignment. She was spoken for before she even arrived in İskenderūn."

"It's hopeless." Tears welled in Ali's eyes. He sniffed and wiped his nose with the back of his hand.

"Take heart," Demetri said. "I managed to find out where she's been taken. She's being held in one of the oldtown houses by the waterfront."

"Then what are we waiting for?" Ali started to slither down the grapevine.

Demetri reached out and halted him. "Wait, we need to think this through. We need a plan. But first things first, we need some food. I don't know about you, but my belly is growling."

Ali shrugged. "I guess so."

Then Demetri suddenly laughed, pointing at Ali.

"What's so funny?"

"Not you," Demetri said, still grinning. "Look, behind you. There's a bird peering right at you."

Ali felt a sudden chill, despite the warmth of the day. He turned to look over his shoulder. Perched on the top of the sandstone wall, barely an arm's length from his face, was an enormous, beady-eyed crow.

The bird let out a loud screech and lunged at him, wings flapping furiously, its pointed black beak aimed straight for his face. Ali sprang sideways, almost toppling, and the bird brushed past him, its talons raking his upper arm.

Demetri said, "What the—"

Then a second, and a third and a fourth crow fell upon them, razor-like beaks and talons slashing. Ali struck out at them and Demetri threw his arms up to protect his face. The birds flapped and darted about them, harrying and attacking the boys.

Ali dropped to the alley, the birds following him. "Come on, Demetri, hurry! We've got to get out of here."

The one-eyed boy half slid, half climbed down the grapevine, lashing out to fend off the crows' frenzied attack.

Suddenly another bird dived, lightning fast and whisper quiet, into the midst of the crows. Ali glimpsed something metallic and rainbow-like, followed by an explosion of squawks and black feathers.

Two of the crows fell bloody and twitching to the ground, and the others took off in all directions.

The avenging newcomer hovered in the air in front of Ali and Demetri for a brief moment—a gemeye about the size of a kingfisher, with large head, prominent beak, iridescent metallic feathers and flashing emerald eyes—before it darted off in pursuit of the fleeing crows.

"Come on!" Ali urged, tugging at Demetri's sleeve.

They took off along the alley, but before they had run even a few metres, a pair of Uzbegs stepped into the entrance, barring their escape.

The boys skidded to a halt and Ali spun about.

Two more Uzbegs were coming along the lane behind them.

"We're trapped," Ali said in alarm.

"Back up the wall," Demetri said, shoving him.

They reached the grapevine and sprang into its tangle of gnarled branches when the sound of thudding horse-hooves heralded the arrival of uniformed cavalry soldiers riding Turkoman battle-mounts. The riders bore down on the Uzbegs, brandishing curved, razor-sharp *kilij* sabres.

With nowhere to turn, the Uzbegs dropped their weapons, their eyes wide.

"Janissaries," Demetri said. "The Sultan's elite fighting troop."

"What are they doing here?" Ali said, staring at them in awe.

The cavalrymen were resplendent in poppy-red, knee-length coats worn over butter-coloured tunics, and *şalvar* trousers tucked into polished red leather boots. They wore distinctive tall, white felt hats, somewhat like stocking caps, with ornamented bronze forehead bands, the stockings folded back like long white tails hanging down their backs.

Demetri shook his head. "No idea. İskenderūn is a long way from the Osmanli capital. And it's supposedly under Mamluk rule. The Janissaries have no authority here."

They reached the top of the wall and peered down. More mounted Janissaries galloped into the compound, wielding steel-tipped lances and riding under a red banner with a single white crescent.

Cries of alarm and outrage rang out from the slavers and their guards.

The commander of the Janissaries surveyed the area, looking down his long aquiline nose, directing his men to round up everyone in the courtyard and herd them into the back corner of the compound. He was a nobleman of considerable stature and bearing, clean-shaven and resplendent in red-braided, daffodil-coloured robes, polished canary-yellow leather boots, and a peacock-blue feathered plume atop his tall white hat.

He spotted Ali and Demetri perched on the wall and reined his mount in their direction. "Hey, you two," he called.

Ali locked eyes with the man and an odd feeling ran through him. The nobleman seemed familiar. But the moment was broken when the clash of steel rang out. A group of slavers and their mercenary guards had taken up arms in a last-ditch effort to escape.

The nobleman reined his horse, unsheathed his jewel-handled *kilij* sabre and turned to join the fray.

"Come on," Ali said. "Let's get out of here. We've got to find Rose."

14. Rose

It was late night and the narrow, cobbled street in the oldtown quarter near the waterfront was dark and quiet.

"Are you sure this is where Rose is being held?" Ali asked.

Demetri scratched his head. "This is the place Abdullah said."

The house was a two-storey sandstone building with a thatched roof. It was huddled shoulder to shoulder with a row of similar houses. What made it different to the others was that its downstairs windows were heavily shuttered.

"There's no way in," Ali said.

They were watching it from a dark edgeway between two buildings across the street. Its single, stout door was bolted and the only sign of life was a faint light shining from a small slit window upstairs.

"Let's have a look around the back," Demetri said.

There were no windows or doors in the rear of the house. In the back yard there was a tall pine tree. Its lower trunk was bare of branches, making it virtually unclimbable, but its vantage was that the high upper limbs overhung the thatched roof of the house.

"I've got an idea," Demetri said. "Follow me."

He led them to the waterfront, where they moved like shadows from one wharf to the next, across dry dock sluices and past boats secured to rusting iron rings set in the stone, searching the moorings.

All was silent, except for the *swish* of waves rolling into shore and the soft thud of boats bumping against pylons. They crept out onto a rickety jetty over the ink-black water that swayed beneath their feet.

"This will do," Ali said, lifting up a coil of hemp mooring-rope with a loop spliced in one end. The other end was tied to a bollard. He hacked it free with his dagger and slung the coil over his shoulder.

"Just what we need," Demetri murmured.

Sidling between stacks of crates and barrels, they left the wharf area and stole back to the house where Rose was supposedly being held.

Ali unslung the coil of rope he had filched from the waterfront, took hold of the looped end, and tried to toss the rest of the coil over one of the upper branches of the tree. The first time it fell short. But he recoiled it, tried again, and it sailed over, the end of the rope snaking back down. Ali threaded the loose end through the loop and pulled the rope tight.

"You don't have to come with me," he whispered. "It might be dangerous."

"I know," Demetri said. "But you might need help."

Ali squeezed his new friend's shoulder in thanks, reached up, took a firm hold of the rope and hauled himself off the ground. Then he locked the rope between his bare feet and inch-wormed his way to the top, where he climbed onto the branch of the tree.

Demetri followed him up, fist over fist. Then they retrieved the rope, climbed out onto the branch and dropped quietly as possible onto the roof of the house. The thatched reeds sagged under their weight and gave off a mouldy, rotten smell. Even by moonlight the roof was in obvious disrepair, thin and holed in places, which suited their purposes well.

They crawled to one of the larger holes and pulled pieces of the thatch away from the edge. When it was large enough, they slipped through the opening and found themselves among a web of rafters and roof struts, looking down into an empty, dimly lit room. The only door into the room was shut. At one end there was a flickering oil lamp on a wooden table, doing little to banish the dark. In the gloom at the other end they could make out an empty sleeping pallet on the floor.

Demetri secured the rope to the beam they were perched on

and lowered it into the room.

Ali indicated Demetri should wait in the rafters, and slid quietly down the rope. As his feet touched the bottom, someone charged at him from the dark back corner of the room.

The attacker hit him low and hard, and even though the unknown person was no larger than Ali himself, the impact and momentum knocked him to the floor. Ali shoved the assailant off him, rolled aside and lurched to his knees. He drew back his fist in preparation to strike, but halted mid-blow.

He blinked in astonishment. "Rose!"

She gasped. "Ali?"

He got to his feet. "Why did you attack me?"

"I heard someone on the roof. I thought..." She tried to gesture with her hands, but they were bound together with thick cord.

Ali wanted to hug her, but instead he unsheathed his dagger and severed her bonds.

She rubbed her wrists. "Thanks, but I would have chewed through them soon anyway."

He grinned, put his dagger away, and helped her to her feet. "Feisty as ever," he said, moving back towards the dangling rope. "Come on, I'll help you up."

But she made no move to follow him.

He went back and tried to take her hand, but she pulled it away.

"What's wrong?" he asked, puzzled.

"What are you doing here, Ali?" She sounded angry, defiant.

"I'm here to help you escape." He couldn't understand why she wasn't excited, grateful.

"Like last time?" she said with derision. "I learned the truth, Ali. Your friend Fedar told me about your little game."

"Game?" Ali frowned in puzzlement. "What's Fedar got to do with this?"

Her green eyes blazed with outrage. "As if you didn't know."

Ali ran his fingers through his hair. "Rose, Fedar is *not* my friend. He's a liar and he was somehow involved in my mother's murder. Not to mention he wants me dead, or worse."

She cocked her head and looked at him. "Then why are you

here? Why are you doing this?"

"Because I can't stop thinking about you," he said. "Because I couldn't bear the thought of you being held prisoner." He paused. Because *I think I love you,* he wanted to say. But instead, he said, "Because I feel responsible for your capture."

Nevertheless, his words disarmed her. The anger faded from her eyes and she studied his face.

The sound of horse hooves suddenly clattered on the cobbles out the front of the building. A door banged open at street level, followed by the sound of voices and footsteps on the stairs.

Rose turned to face the door and took up a defensive fighting stance: one foot a little in front, the other turned aside, half crouched and ready to spring, her fists raised.

"Quick, lay back down," Ali whispered. "Let's not show our hand to soon. Pretend you're asleep."

Her gaze flicked from him to the door. She moved hesitantly back to the sleeping pallet.

Ali grabbed the coarse rope and climbed hurriedly back into the rafters. Demetri hauled it back up behind him.

The door burst open and two figures entered the room.

Ali shifted slightly to steady his balance, and the beam they were perched on lurched and cracked under his weight. He glanced anxiously down to see if he had been seen or heard, only to suppress a gasp of recognition when the two men moved into the lamplight.

The largest of the pair was Khasis, the full-bearded Uzbeg. He now wore a studded leather jerkin in place of his chainmail and armour. He plonked a bottle of wine and a clay cup onto the table and slumped onto one of the chairs, adjusting his sword so he could sit comfortably.

The other person was none other than Fedar himself, swathed in his familiar magenta cloak, his black felt *kalpak* perched on his head.

Ali's mouth fell open and he felt suddenly cold.

"You let the boy slip out of your grasp," Fedar said, closing the door to the room.

Khasis poured himself a slug of wine and took a large gulp.

"What could my men do against a troop of mounted Janissaries?"

Fedar pursed his lips. "I'll admit, that was unexpected. As far as I knew the Janissaries were all but wiped out by Timur Lenk's army in the Battle of Ankara."

Khasis cursed. "These weren't just Janissaries, they were the elite cavalry. What's more, they were led by Omar Agha himself."

Fedar looked across at where Rose lay still on the pallet at the other end of the room. Ali went rigid with dread, afraid the skull-faced old man would spy them in the shadows of the rafters.

"It's dangerous with Ali on the loose," Fedar said.

Khasis gave a sneer. "My men will get him."

Fedar snorted. "Without the help of my crows your men would still be looking for him in Korykos."

Khasis took another swig of wine. "We'll get him next time."

"You'd better. Now put that wine aside. We've got to take this girl to Prince Savich tonight. I want her bound and gagged. You can carry her down and put her in the back of my carriage."

Khasis scowled. "Why not just wait until tomorrow after we snatch this David, the other dreamer, in Aşkarbeyli?"

"Hi name's Davud," Fedar said. "Davud bin Abdullah."

"Makes no sense leaving tonight, then coming all the way back tomorrow," Khasis said.

Fedar spoke through his teeth with forced restraint. "We have to take her tonight. Prince Savich needs her to bait his trap for Erkan Pasha. The timing is crucial. I told you."

"Yes, *you* told me," Khasis said belligerently. "But how do I know that's what Savich Çelebi actually said? I didn't hear him, did I? You claim he communicates with you in your mind, but how do I know that?"

Fedar took two long strides to the table and leaned over, his face close to Khasis' own. "Do you doubt Prince Savich's ability?" he said in a low voice.

Despite his superior size and strength, Khasis shrank back. "No, of course not. I…ah… I just think it makes more sense to wait until tomorrow."

Ali turned and looked at Demetri in alarm. He dared not breathe for fear of being heard. His mind reeled: there was another dreamer? They were taking Rose to the man they called Prince Savich.

"Get the girl organised," Fedar ordered.

Khasis banged his wine cup on to the table and rose to his feet. He farted and gave Fedar a sneer, then took a length of cord from inside his studded leather jerkin and advanced towards Rose.

As he approached the pallet, Rose jack-knifed to her feet and charged at him, her fingernails raking at his face.

"Guards!" Fedar yelled.

Khasis struck her a back-handed blow that made her teeth *clack* and sent her sprawling.

She crumpled on the floor and sobbed.

Ali shifted his weight and the beam they were on suddenly gave a loud, splintering crack and snapped in half, dumping him and Demetri unceremoniously onto the floor of the room.

15. Prisoners

Khasis leapt into action before Ali and Demetri could recover themselves. He grabbed Rose by the hair with one hand and whipped out his sword with the other. "Don't move a muscle," he snarled, thrusting the point of his blade at the boys' faces, "or I'll stick you like lambs."

Heavy footsteps clattered on the stairs.

Fedar rubbed his bony hands and leered. "Gifts from heaven."

"I told you we'd get him," Khasis said, laughing.

Rose kicked at the Uzbeg but he sidestepped and flung her to the floor alongside Ali and Demetri.

Three Uzbeg mercenaries barrelled into the room.

"Bind them," Fedar ordered.

The guards confiscated the boys' daggers and bound both them and Rose securely before dragging them all into the centre of the room.

Fedar came and leaned over Ali, his skull-like face close, his lip curled in a sneer. "You've led us on a merry chase, my boy. That was an interesting little trick you pulled back in Korykos. It almost worked. Almost…"

Fedar stood and paced the room.

Khasis moved back to the table, poured himself another cup of wine.

"We have a problem," Fedar said, wringing his hands again.

Ali stopped squirming and pricked his ears. A problem for Fedar might mean an opportunity for them.

Khasis took a swig of wine and cursed. "What do you mean?"

"I have to take the girl to Savich tonight," Fedar said.

"So?" Khasis said, shrugging.

"It means you'll have to stay here and guard these two," Fedar said, gesturing at Ali and Demetri.

"Just bring them with us," Khasis said, banging down his cup.

Fedar shook his head. "Too dangerous. We can't risk upsetting Savich's plan."

Khasis lurched to his feet. "I'm not staying here alone with him. What if he—"

"Hold your tongue!" Fedar snapped. "All you have to do is watch them."

Khasis cracked his knuckles and glared at Fedar. "I don't like it."

"I don't like it either, but we haven't got any choice." Fedar walked over and prodded Ali in the ribs with his toe. "Just keep this one awake and he'll be as harmless as the other one."

Khasis raised his wine cup and drained it. "When will you be back?"

Fedar moved to the door. "All going well, in a couple of days."

"What about the other dreamer in Aşkarbeyli?" Khasis asked, his brow furrowed.

"We'll get him when I return. In the meantime, just watch these two closely." Fedar stabbed his finger at Khasis. "And make that your last cup of wine."

Fedar gave a signal and one of the Uzbeg guards scooped Rose up and slung her over his shoulder.

"Ali," she screamed, kicking and writhing.

Ali bucked and strained at his bonds. "Rose!"

Beside him, Demetri twisted and pulled at his bindings.

Fedar strode out the door and down the stairs, followed by the burly Uzbeg guard carrying the squirming Rose.

"*No,*" Ali cried, his muscles jumping under his skin.

Khasis drew his sword and advanced on the two boys. "Shut up," he said, kicking Ali in the ribs. He stood over them for a moment, glowering. Then when he heard the sound of horses moving off along the street he returned to his seat at the table and poured himself yet another cup of wine.

"Keep watch downstairs," he told the two remaining guards, who trooped off at his order.

Khasis sat drinking alone at the table, despite Fedar's instruction to lay off the wine. But every so often he got to his feet and came over to give Ali a nudge to make sure he was awake, to make sure he could not dream.

The irony was, Ali had not been able to dream his prophetic, future-shaping dreams since he had escaped from Fedar's workroom in Korykos. Back then he had wanted to get rid of the dreams, and now when he wanted to use them he was unable.

Khasis started on a second bottle of wine, and as the night wore on he stopped coming over quite so frequently to nudge Ali. Eventually the wine had a soporific effect on the hefty Uzbeg and he nodded off to sleep slumped in his chair, snoring loudly.

Ali and Demetri made silent signals to each other and tried to loosen their bonds, but they were securely bound. Without their daggers or some other sharp implement, it was hopeless. Demetri eventually gave in to sleep, and after a while Ali felt himself dozing off from exhaustion.

Then he began to dream…

A red-tinged dream.

Ali pictured a face. The face of the aquiline-nosed nobleman he had seen at the head of the Royal Janissaries at the slave market. The man whose gaze had pierced Ali's very being. Once again he was at the head of a troop of cavalry, elite disciplined fighting men. But this time, instead of approaching the slave market, the mounted troops were approaching the house in which Ali and Demetri were prisoners.

In the dream the Janissaries reined to a halt in the street—

Ali jerked suddenly awake, gasping. His mouth was filled with the taste of copper, but his face was wet with vinegary red wine. He blinked it from his eyes and looked up.

Khasis was standing over him, red-faced, a vein throbbing in his temple, an empty wine cup in his hand. "Wake up," he roared. He cursed Ali and gave him a kick for good measure.

Ali grunted in pain.

Before long, there was a commotion downstairs. Men were

yelling and there came a loud crash that made the building shake. Khasis snarled and drew his sword, lurching down the stairs.

"What's happening?" Demetri said, rubbing his eyes.

The clang of steel and the sound of angry voices came from downstairs.

"The Janissaries are here," Ali said.

Demetri scratched his cheek. "How…?"

Ali allowed himself a small grin. "They must have already been here in İskenderūn, but I think my dream guided them to this place to rescue us."

"Your dream?" Demetri frowned. "What do you mean?"

Ali gazed at the roof, thinking about how to word it. "Remember when I told you I have something they want? Something I couldn't tell you about. It's an ability. My dreams have power."

Demetri inclined his head and frowned. "I don't understand."

But before Ali could explain further, Khasis suddenly came bounding back up the stairs, blood running down his face from a deep cut across his cheek. He halted a moment, his sword wavering, then advanced upon Ali with a wild look in his eyes.

Ali squirmed in his bindings, never taking his gaze from Khasis' sword point. The man raised the blade two-handed in preparation to strike. Ali tensed, his chest tight. He thought of Rose, realising there was nothing he could do now to help her. At least Fedar wouldn't be able to control his dreams. He closed his eyes, expecting to feel the deadly bite of cold steel.

But instead, Khasis gave a deep grunt and his weapon clattered to the floor. Ali opened his eyes and saw the bloodied point of a lance protruding from the wide-eyed Uzbeg's chest. Khasis tottered, a gurgling sound issuing from his throat, red bubbles flecking his lips, then he collapsed to the floor with a heavy thud and was still.

In the doorway stood the dark-eyed nobleman from the company of Royal Janissaries, and Ali knew with certainty that his dreams had returned.

"You two?" the nobleman said with a double-take. "I saw you at the slave auction. What are you doing here? Why are you being held prisoner?"

The nobleman withdrew a curved-bladed knife from his belt, knelt beside Ali and Demetri, and sawed at their bindings until they parted.

Ali got to his feet and helped Demetri up.

"We came here to rescue a girl but we were captured," Ali said, rubbing his wrists to restore the circulation.

The nobleman grabbed Ali by the arm and shook him. "What girl? My daughter, the Lady Ashye?"

"A slave girl," Demetri said. "No high-born lady, my Lord."

"A friend of mine named Rose," Ali said.

A Janissary officer clattered up the steps and saluted the nobleman. "I'm afraid the Lady Ashye is nowhere to be found, sir."

The nobleman released his grip on Ali. He pinched his aquiline nose and sighed deeply with grim resignation. "Thank you, Captain. Have some men take the prisoners to the temporary barracks for questioning. I'll be along shortly."

He removed his tall, feather-plumed white felt hat and rubbed his fingers through his thick, dark hair. He turned wearily to face Ali and Demetri and said, "I am Omar Agha."

Ali and Demetri looked at each other. The name meant nothing to them.

"I am the Agha, the General of the Amasya Janissaries, for His Majesty Sultan Mehmed Çelebi."

The boys' eyes went wide. "What are you doing here in İskenderūn?" Ali asked. "This city is under Mamluk rule. Surely you risk war just showing your faces."

"I am searching for my daughter," the Agha said. "She has been kidnapped. My informers told me she was being held here in İskenderūn. But my search stalled when we did not find her at the slave market. Then just now, a strange compulsion brought me to this house, an urgent call, a picture in my mind. I think that these, these Uzbegs," he spat the name like a swear word, "may have held her prisoner here. Have you seen any sign of her?"

Ali and Demetri both shook their heads.

Despite this the Agha continued. "I am offering a significant reward for information that helps me find her. If you know something please tell me. You are free now. I hold no claim over you. But I beg of you, if you know something, anything, you must tell me."

"We haven't seen anyone here except Rose," Ali said.

"What happened to her?" the Agha asked.

"They took her to someone they called Prince Savich," Ali said.

"*Savich!*" The Agha grasped Ali by his shoulders, the man's fingers digging into his flesh. "Where?"

"They didn't say," Ali said. "Who is this Savich? Why would they be taking Rose to him?"

The Agha released his grip on Ali. "When Sultan Bayezid died a prisoner in Timur Lenk's cells, Timur himself appointed Bayezid's son Mehmed as Sultan. It was a good choice. Of all the princes he would make the best, fairest and just ruler. I pledged my allegiance to him."

"With respect," Demetri said, "that's history. Who is this Savich and what has he to do with Bayezid and Mehmed?"

"When Timur Lenk himself died attempting to conquer China, his rule in Anatolia collapsed and the splintered Osmanli empire erupted into civil war. Brother against brother, each wanting to be Sultan. They're still fighting now. Savich, the usurper, is trying to take advantage of this instability to take over himself."

"The Uzbegs are working for him?" asked Ali.

The Agha nodded. "He has enlisted mercenaries from Timur Lenk's vast force to create his own army."

Ali frowned as an idea popped into his head. "Why would Savich want Rose?"

"I don't know," the Agha said. "All I know is that Savich has taken my daughter to help legitimise his claim to the throne. I can't let him do that."

"Is it possible," Ali asked, "that Rose and the Lady Ashye are one and the same?"

The Agha looked askance at Ali, but scratched his chin thoughtfully. "What does your friend Rose look like?"

Ali closed his eyes and pictured her in his mind. "Medium height. Green eyes—"

"Green eyes! What else?" the Agha asked.

"Short, raven-black hair."

The Agha shook his head. "The Lady Ashye has long brown hair." He turned to Demetri. "Why did you say your friend was no high-born lady?"

"She speaks like someone from the streets," Demetri replied. "Not cultured and formal like you, my Lord. And she dressed in a simple, well-worn peasant kaftan."

"Then we are talking about two different people," the Agha said. "Did you hear anything else that might help me?"

"Only that Savich's men are setting a trap for someone called Erkan Pasha," Ali said.

"The Sultan's Vizir! When? How?"

Ali shrugged. "That's all I know."

The Agha clapped him on the back. "Thank you. Time is running out, I must go."

"Please," Ali implored, "can I ask you for help?"

"What is it?"

"I fear time is running out for my friend, Rose, too. In your hunt for your daughter will you also look for her? Rescue her too if you can? You and your Janissaries might be her only hope."

"Fair enough. My daughter comes first, but I will also help your friend if I find her." He turned with a swirl of his finely embroidered cloak and left.

"Why didn't you tell the Agha about this Davud person in Aşkarbeyli?" Demetri asked. "Fedar called him a *Dreamer*. Is he like you? What's with this dreaming thing?"

Ali gave a small nod of resignation. "You asked me the other day why the Uzbegs were after me. I think it's time I told you what's going on."

"It might help," Demetri said, clasping his hands under his chin in a prayer gesture.

"Let's get out of here first," Ali said. "Who knows if there are more Uzbegs around. And what if Fedar was to return unexpectedly?"

They retrieved their daggers and departed the old sandstone house that had been Rose's prison, making their way to the waterfront where they found a street vendor selling buttermilk from a cart. There, sipping clay cups of the sour, creamy drink,

Ali told him everything. About his dreams, about Hasan. About Big-hands. About Rose. His treatment by Fedar, how he escaped. And how he dreamed their rescue by the Agha and his Janissaries.

Demetri listened without uttering a word.

"You must think I am crazy," Ali said.

Demetri blinked. "I don't know what to say. Your story is fantastic but the pieces seem to fit. What about this Davud? Where does he fit in? Can he do what you do?"

"That's what I want to find out," Ali said. "I'm hoping he can help me learn more about my dreams, and whether I can use them to save Rose."

"And if he can't help you?" Demetri asked.

Ali set his jaw and clenched his fists. "Then I'll warn him about Fedar and the Uzbegs and I'll continue east to find Rose."

"But the Agha has captured the Uzbegs. Surely this Davud has nothing to fear now?"

Ali shook his head. "You don't understand. There are complexities at work here I can only guess at. I think Davud is in great danger."

Demetri gave him an apprehensive look.

Ali punched him lightly on the arm. "Come on, it's time to get out of here. If you're still with me let's make our way to Aşkarbeyli village and see if we can find this Davud."

"I'm with you all the way," Demetri said.

16. Wild Dreaming

It was late morning by the time Ali and Demetri trudged up the dusty main street of Aşkarbeyli. The village was perched in the hills to the east of İskenderūn, set among market gardens and groves of lemon, orange and ripe almond trees, overlooking the city and the bay in the distance. The surrounding hills were forested with pines and plane trees.

Ali and Demetri made their way to the market square where a small crowd was gathered expectantly around one of the stalls, joking and talking. They stepped around an old woman squatting on a rug piled high with crimson-red pomegranates, and pushed their way through the crowd to find a flustered man and woman in the stall, both wearing long, quilted pine needle-green robes, arguing with each other in a foreign tongue.

"Who are they?" Demetri asked the man, a honey-seller, standing next to him.

"They're Kazakhs," the man said. "Steppe nomads who fled here via Anatolia after Timur Lenk conquered the Golden Horde in their homeland. They breed those huge *Dzhabe* horses up in the hills and peddle their foodstuffs here in the market."

Ali peered at the stallholders' offerings: steaming bowls of stewed meat and flat noodles, and clay cups of a milky-looking drink. Large, unglazed ceramic bottles sealed with wax were lined up behind the pair on a trestle table at the rear of the stall.

"The drink is *kumis*," the honey-seller said, offering them his clay cup. "It's fermented mare's milk. Have a taste, it's good. And the food is *beshbarmak*, made from boiled horse meat."

Ali took the cup and had a sip. It was creamy and it fizzed a little in his mouth, leaving a foamy, sour aftertaste.

"Why the crowd?" asked Demetri, taking the cup from Ali and trying the Kazakhs' drink. He pulled a *yuck* face and handed it back to Ali.

The man pointed towards a woman and a boy sitting a short distance away on a log under a shady evergreen cedar tree. "The young soothsayer is demonstrating his abilities."

"What do you mean?" Ali asked.

Before the man could reply, a loud *pop* rang out from inside the Kazakhs' stall.

The crowd cheered.

Ali turned to see a fountain of *kumis* erupting from the neck of one of the large ceramic bottles in the rear of the stall.

"That's three," someone yelled.

A group of people surged around the boy and the woman sitting under the cedar.

"That's the third bottle to pop," the honey-seller said, scratching his head. "The boy was right. Who would credit it? It's never happened before."

"I don't understand," Ali said, handing back the man's cup.

"The Kazakhs brought a new batch of *kumis* to the market this morning and the boy correctly predicted three of the bottles would explode before morning's end." The man accepted his cup back. "Now that he's proved he can see the future, he's telling fortunes and I want to get in line."

Ali and Demetri followed the man and joined the queue waiting to consult with the boy. Ali assumed this was the other dreamer Savich and Khasis had spoken of, the one they called Davud. But he could not be certain until they met and spoke. As each person stepped up to face the young fortune-teller, the woman beside him collected the payment, which she tucked into an embroidered purse on her lap.

The woman wore a sheer white veil over her dark, curly hair, the end of which she held pulled across her face. Beneath it her face was lined and wrinkled, her eyes a piercing, pale grey. She was dressed in a long, dark jacket over a shorter maroon top and a pair of loose white-and-blue-striped pants that ballooned at the ankles. The boy wore a pale-red cap and a raw cotton kaftan and baggy pants.

When it was Ali's turn the woman held out her hand and said in a surprisingly youthful voice, "A silver coin for each question you want to ask."

"I come offering counsel, not seeking it," Ali said.

"Pay your money or move along," the boy said in an off-handed, arrogant manner.

"If you're called Davud," Demetri said, leaning around Ali, "I think you should listen to my friend. We know about your dreams."

The boy started to speak but the woman silenced him with a sharp look and got to her feet.

"That's all for today," she announced loudly to the waiting people. "My son is weary. Please come back tomorrow afternoon. Your questions will be answered and the future revealed. Thank you."

At first there were some mutterings and complaints at this premature end to the proceedings, but soon the remaining people dispersed and made their way back to the market.

When the stragglers were out of earshot the woman turned to face Ali and Demetri. "If it's money you're after, you can forget it. We have no need of your advice."

"My advice is free," Ali said. Then he turned and made eye contact with Davud. "I know you are a dreamer. It's not safe for you here, you must leave."

"Not safe," the woman said, sneering. "If you know so much about my son, you must realise he has the power to protect us."

"All I know is that your son is in danger." Ali pointed to himself. "I too have dreams, dreams of the future. And because of this I have been manipulated, hunted and held prisoner. We escaped only this morning and came straight here to warn you."

Davud looked at his mother in alarm but she cut him off again with a glare and turned back to Ali. "You dream?"

"Yes," Ali said, "I do."

"So you come to challenge my son?" she said accusingly.

Ali's brow wrinkled in a frown. "Challenge? What are you

talking about? I came here to warn you. There are men planning to come here and capture you. Among them there is a man called Fedar who would use alchemy and sorcery to control your son's dreams."

"Is this some sort of trick?" Davud asked, his tone scornful. "Pretending there is danger to put me off guard? Your tactics are—"

Davud's mother held up her hand and the boy fell silent. "My name is Fatma," she said in a friendlier manner. "Fatma bint Abdullah. I am Davud's mother. How did you learn about my son, know that he dreams?"

"We overheard our captors plotting to come here and capture you," Ali said.

Her pale grey eyes went wide behind the veil. "To capture *us?*"

Ali nodded. "Our escape will have disrupted their immediate plans, but if I know Fedar, he will still come, or at least send someone. Possibly as soon as tomorrow or the day after."

Fatma considered him for a moment, then inclined her head in thanks. "We will leave first thing in the morning."

"I think that's wise," Ali said.

"It's getting late and you must be tired and hungry," she said. "Please eat with us, stay the night at the inn and tell us more of your ordeal."

"But we have no money," Demetri said.

"We will pay," Fatma said kindly. She patted her purse. "We have plenty of money. As you have seen, our little sideshow is more than just a way to pass the time of day."

Fatma took them to a walled garden behind the inn where they had lodgings. She ordered a dish of spicy *alinazik pilav* to share, a stew of smoked eggplant, grilled lamb and rice. As he ate, Ali told them about Fedar and Rose and his escape from Korykos. He warned them about the crows and the Uzbegs, and about Fedar wanting to control their dreams. Fatma and Davud hung on his every word, questioning him over this detail or that—especially about his dreams. They were perfect hosts, attentive, friendly and generous.

Demetri, on the other hand, remained silent and watchful throughout the meal.

"What was wrong with you?" Ali asked when they retired to their room.

Demetri bolted the door. "I don't trust them, Ali. Something's not quite right here. Can't you feel it?"

Ali shook his head. "He's a dreamer like me. They're the first people I've met who understand what I'm going through. They're our friends."

"They sound too good to be true. And what was that business about a challenge? There's something they're not telling us."

"They just thought we were going to muscle in on their little game."

Demetri moved across to his sleeping pallet. "Maybe. Maybe not. But I don't trust them."

Ali laughed and flopped on to his pallet. "All right, I'll be careful. Now let's get some sleep, I'm exhausted."

Ali put his head down and closed his eyes and before long he had fallen into a deep sleep. A sleep in which he soon began to dream. A vividly realistic dream which felt similar to one of his red-tinged foretelling dreams, but was also completely different to any dream he had ever had before.

His mouth was filled with the familiar coppery dream taste, but the dream was devoid of all colour, the details rendered in greenish shades of black and white. What's more, he sensed that the outcome of the dream was uncertain and that he was still under threat, that this dream was some sort of contest. But the most remarkable thing about the dream was that it was not his alone.

Whether it had been Demetri's mention of Davud's "challenge" that started him dreaming, or whether it was some sort of survival instinct, Ali did not know. But he and Davud must have begun dreaming at the same time, and somehow they were both in the *same* dream:

Ali found himself walking side by side with Davud along a dusty street on the outskirts of İskenderūn. Davud quickened his pace and Ali lengthened his own stride to keep up. Then Davud shot him a black glare and took off at a run. Ali realised that he was racing towards a golden light coming from a man standing at the far end of the street.

He wondered fleetingly how he had failed to notice the man. Everything else in the dream was grey except for the man's glowing image, resplendent in golden robes and illuminated by a shining aura around his head. He shone like the sun. But everyone else on the street—children playing, a woman carrying a wooden yoke strung with crates of chickens, and even a stooped, heavily bearded Wandering Pilgrim shuffling along the roadside—were faded and colourless.

Ali realised that he and Davud were opponents, racing each other to reach the illuminated man. A man who shone so brightly that Ali reasoned he could be none other than Luman himself, the legendary source of light and wisdom.

Both Ali's own mother and the peculiar sailor had urged Ali to seek Luman, and now it looked like Davud might reach the revered man ahead of him.

Ali pushed himself harder, straining muscles and tendons until he gradually closed the gap. He came up alongside Davud, racing neck and neck, but he could not draw ahead.

Then Davud lunged and shoved him aside.

Ali stumbled out of control, half running, half falling. The figure of the Wandering Pilgrim suddenly loomed before him. Ali cried a warning, but it was too late. He collided with the hapless man and the two of them tumbled together in the dust.

Davud bellowed a victory cry and raced towards the shining man at the end of the street.

Strangely, Ali felt no loss, no defeat. Instead he felt only fear and concern for the Wandering Pilgrim lying in the dust beside him. Ignoring his own injuries and pain, which felt as palpable to him as if they had happened in real life rather than a dream, he gave up on his desire to beat Davud, to reach the illuminated man ahead of his rival, and turned instead to help the fallen man.

All of a sudden the dream was painted with a red tinge, and Ali sensed it now belonged to him alone. He was no longer sharing the dreamscape with his adversary.

17. The Wandering Pilgrim

Ali woke in the morning to find Demetri already up and about, peering furtively out of the small window of their room.

"What's wrong?" Ali said.

"We have to leave." Demetri moved to the door, opened it a fraction and peeked out before easing it shut again. "There's an Uzbeg nosing around downstairs and your friends Davud and Fatma have gone; they left before sunrise."

Ali got to his feet. "You were right about those two, Demetri. They are no friends of mine."

Demetri scratched his temple. "That's not what you said last night."

"They were putting on a charade." Ali pulled on his vest. "I shared a dream with Davud last night. We both dreamed the same dream. It was a contest of sorts, his will against mine in a race for Luman."

"Luman!" Demetri's eyes went wide. "What happened?"

"I'm not sure. The dream ended before the final act. I expect the conclusion will unfold today."

Demetri's mouth fell open. "Today! Are you prepared for it?"

Ali shrugged, but his stomach gave a nervous flutter. "Come on, let's get out of here."

They crept out of their room and down the stairs on tiptoes. At the bottom they paused and peeked into the common room. The Uzbeg had his back to them, watching the entrance to the inn. They slipped quickly and quietly out the back door and ran for the cover of a tall wheatgrass clump. Keeping an eye out for watching crows, they skirted through the surrounding brushland back to the İskenderūn road where they managed to hitch a ride with a chicken farmer.

It was a noisy and uncomfortable journey, crouched in the back of his cart between cages of squawking hens, but as Ali pointed out, it kept them hidden from prying eyes. The chicken farmer dropped them off in the livestock market around midday amid bleating goats, the odour of chicken shit and warm animal dung.

"What now?" Demetri asked, plucking downy brown and white feathers from his hair and clothes.

"You go and get something to eat," Ali replied. "I have a strong feeling I'm destined to be somewhere else if ever I'm to find Luman, learn about my dreams and rescue Rose. All going well, I'll meet you later back at Lemon Tree."

Demetri clapped his hand on Ali's shoulder. "I'm coming with you."

Ali shook his head. "Thank you, my friend, but no. This is something I must do on my own. I have dreamed of this already and you weren't part of it."

Demetri gave a small nod of understanding. "Then I'll be with you in spirit."

Ali gave him a sad smile and turned away to stride out of the market.

He went instinctively east, wondering at first where he was going, but gradually gaining confidence he was on the right path. Certain roads felt right, left him with a warm feeling in his gut. After some time, he saw Davud coming towards him from the opposite direction. Midway between them was a crossroad. For a brief moment their eyes met, Davud's gaze stony cold, then they both reached the intersection and turned into the north-bound street.

It was the street from their shared dream.

They walked shoulder to shoulder, barely acknowledging each other—the moves already laid down, unchangeable. The only difference was that this time Ali was aware of other sensations he had not noticed in the dream: sounds, smells, even the crunch and feel of the gravel on the road underfoot.

Davud started to run and Ali increased his own stride to keep up with him, exactly as they had dreamed. They ran neck and neck, straining, breathing hard.

Ali saw the children playing, heard their joyful laughter, saw the woman with the chickens, and recognised the Wandering Pilgrim. Then he saw the man who must be Luman standing in a sphere of bright light at the end of the street.

Could he really be the immortal sage of old? The servant of Tengri, the source of light and wellbeing? The one who could solve all Ali's problems?

Then Davud lunged at him.

Ali ducked and swerved, but the blow caught him all the same. He stumbled out of control, fighting to keep his balance. The pilgrim loomed in front of him—

"Look out!" Ali cried.

They collided, tumbled, and sprawled in the dust, taunted by the sound of Davud's triumphant victory cry.

Ali looked up in time to see Davud rushing jubilantly towards the figure of the golden man. The figure he assumed was Luman, the object of his quest. Logic told him that he had lost, but strangely he did not feel like a loser. Instead he felt sadness for Davud and compassion for the hapless Wandering Pilgrim he had bowled over.

"I'm terribly sorry, pilgrim. Are you all right? Do you hurt anywhere?" Ali climbed to his feet and took the man under his arms, lifting him into a sitting position.

"Yes, yes," croaked the gnarled pilgrim, his moustache quivering. "I'm all right. Give me your hand."

Ali helped him to his feet, dusting his grey kaftan so vigorously that a cloud of dust threatened to envelop them both.

The old man coughed. "That's enough, boy. Stop it, I said I'm all right. Next thing you'll have me sneezing. Mischief-maker, I'm surprised you even bothered to stop for me. Your friend didn't. What's the hurry, eh?" His voice had a sharp edge, but his eyes were warm, gentle.

"He's not my friend." Ali's face flushed with embarrassment.

"We were competing, racing to reach the golden man."

"Ha. What golden man? I see no golden man."

Ali looked along the street. Davud had almost reached the end, but Ali could no longer see the illuminated man.

"Why were you seeking such a man?" the pilgrim asked, thoughtfully stroking his moustache.

"I thought he was Luman. I was seeking his help."

"Ha, Luman!" The Wandering Pilgrim's moustache bristled. "Why did you bother to stop for me if you were on such an important quest?"

"Because I knocked you down, *efendi*. I couldn't leave you in the gutter." Ali began to dust the old man again.

The Wandering Pilgrim took Ali's hands in his own and stilled them. He peered searchingly into Ali's face. "Yes you could—your friend left me."

"But I was the one who collided with you…"

"Ha! I saw what happened, boy, there is no need to explain. So, you seek the legendary Luman, the servant of Tengri?" He gave Ali a quizzical smile.

Ali swallowed and nodded.

"Then believe me, that was not Luman."

"But the golden man? I thought…"

"Ha. The golden man was the other boy's image, not yours. His was based on greed and selfish desire. Look, there never was a golden man."

The Wandering Pilgrim pointed to the end of the street where Davud had thrown his arms around the neck of a donkey and was smothering the bewildered animal with kisses.

"Ha. That is his golden man." The Wandering Pilgrim gave a low chuckle. "He will soon realise his mistake, so it would be best if you are not around when he does."

"But what about Luman?"

"Only the pure of heart can find the true Luman, and to do so they must follow the Lost River and travel the Forgotten Way to Bādiyah Ash-Shām. Luman is in the desert, everyone knows that. But few know to take the Forgotten Way."

"The Forgotten Way?"

"Look for it east of the Bird Boulders. It's the ancient way, the pilgrim's way, into the heart of Bādiyah Ash-Shām. Now, quickly, begone before your besotted friend realises his folly."

18. The Lost River

The sun was sinking in the west by the time Ali found his way back to the Lemon Tree. He entered the common room, inhaling the familiar yeasty odour of *boza,* and called to Demetri, who was squatting by the fireplace stirring the steaming contents of a communal soup pot.

The one-eyed boy gave Ali a look of relief and stood to embrace him. "I was getting worried about you. There have been stories of Uzbeg activity around the city all day. What happened? Did you find Luman?"

Ali grimaced and shook his head.

Demetri's expression fell. "You lost?"

"No," Ali said thoughtfully. "But I'm not sure I won either. It turns out the golden man wasn't Luman after all, just a dream image created by Davud. But I met a Wandering Pilgrim who told me how to find the real Luman."

Demetri ladled a bowl of *mercimek çorbasi,* the local lentil soup, from the pot and passed it to him. "Here, have some of this. It's surprisingly good. What did the pilgrim say?"

Ali blew on the hot soup. "He told me to find the Lost River and the Forgotten Way."

"I know where the Lost River is, it's east of here, at the foot of Mount Simeon. But I've never heard of this Forgotten Way. The forgotten way to where?"

"To the desert, Bādiyah Ash-Shām."

"Oh, is *that* all," Demetri said with a note of sarcasm. "If you don't die of hunger and thirst, the snakes or scorpions will probably get you! You have to watch out for them. Nine out of ten people who go there never come back, you know."

Ali took a gulp of soup, chewing the chunks of carrots, potatoes and onions in the thick red lentil broth. "Unless they are Bedouin," he said in grim agreement.

"We'll need to pool our money and get provisions from the market for the journey," Demetri said.

"We?" Ali said.

Demetri planted his feet wide and lifted his chin. "I'm coming with you this time. I won't be left behind again."

"It's too dangerous, you said as much yourself."

Demetri shrugged. "It's dangerous for me here too now. Fedar could be back any time."

"I thought you were going to Greece?"

"To be honest, I'm not sure any more about going to Greece. I've been here in İskenderūn for almost a year. I could have found a way to Greece during that time, but when you think about it, for some reason I've been travelling east instead of west. Consciously or unconsciously, I've not only delayed going to Greece, I've been travelling further away from it. I have no family there anymore. My grandparents are long dead. And I've heard that they don't look kindly upon us Anatolian Greeks. They call us half-Greek and scorn us, so I'm not sure life would be any better for me there."

"What are you going to do then?"

"It's obvious, isn't it? I'm coming with you."

Ali gave his friend a grateful nod and sipped his soup.

They set off early the next morning, both wearing cloaks with the hoods pulled low over their faces. Ali still had the dark-green cloak Jemal had given him, and they had pooled the last of their cash to buy one for Demetri. In addition, they each had a small sack packed with dried fruit and nuts, and a waterskin. Ali also had a tinder pouch and candle in his that Demetri had "found" somewhere.

They walked steadily, uphill most of the way, without any sign of trouble until around midday. When they stopped and sat on a log to eat lunch, Demetri suddenly grabbed Ali's leg.

"Don't look now," he said in a low voice, "but there are a pair of crows in that tall plane tree across the road."

Ali pulled the cloak lower over his face. "Have they recognised us?"

"I don't think so," Demetri said. "But they're curious."

"Fedar must've found out we escaped and sent them to search for us." He stood. "Let's keep moving."

They reached the Lost River as dusk was falling. They had sighted more crows during the afternoon, and both had the peculiar feeling they were being watched, but their journey was otherwise incident free. The warm evening was buzzing with insects. They made camp in a clearing surrounded by sage bushes, which Demetri said would keep the bugs away, and ate a meal of almonds and dried apricots before wrapping themselves in their cloaks and going to sleep.

That was when things took a turn for the worse. Ali's sleep was invaded by a nightmare like nothing he had ever experienced.

He dreamed of a faceless man: an ominous dark figure without features except for two coal-black pits where his eyes should have been. Despite having no mouth, the man called to Ali, called him by name, seductively, like a Siren.

The voice was bewitching, compelling, but it felt wrong, and Ali knew instinctively he had to resist. He writhed and twitched in his sleep, groaning and shivering with the effort.

The faceless figure laughed and called, "come to me," even though he had no mouth.

"No," Ali moaned, soaked in sweat.

The faceless man continued his relentless call, on and on, snickering with barely suppressed mirth, trying to wear Ali down, to erode his defences.

Ali woke with the sunrise, exhausted. The effort of resisting the faceless man had left him drained. It had taken every bit of strength he had to withstand the pull of his beckoning call.

He stood, yawned and stretched, and woke Demetri.

They scanned the trees for crows, and were relieved to find no sign of them. For breakfast they ate more nuts and dried fruit.

When Demetri heard about Ali's nightmare and how it had left him feeling, he brewed some sage tea over a small fire.

"It will help you feel better, dispel your dark mood, plus they say it's good for your stomach," Demetri said.

"There's nothing wrong with my stomach," Ali laughed. But he sipped the tea gratefully. It was an aromatic, slightly bitter brew and Demetri was right: whether it was the tea or mind over matter, he soon felt better

After breakfast, they broke camp and made their way down to the river bank.

"Why is it called the Lost River?" Ali asked, gazing at the wide expanse of water.

Demetri chuckled. "Because it disappears and nobody can explain where it goes."

Ali studied the river. It came gushing and foaming down from the hills to the north-east, falling over a rocky ledge in a plume of white water, before slowing and broadening into a wide sedate river. It flowed along like that for some way, past where he and Demetri had camped for the night, until finally it ran into a low-lying area further to the south.

Then it simply stopped, vanished. There was no white water, no waterfall or whirlpool, no lake. Beyond the end of the river the land climbed in a series of craggy hills stretching all the way to distant Mount Simeon.

Ali gawked at it in amazement.

"People have dived down to the bottom of the river looking for a hole," Demetri said. "But they found nothing. Some say the ground is porous and the water dissolves into the centre of the Earth, but no-one really knows."

"The Wandering Pilgrim told me we should look for the Forgotten Way east of the Bird Boulders," Ali said.

Demetri pointed to a series of balancing rocks which jutted from the forest in the hills above them. "That's them up there."

Ali gave the Lost River one last, thoughtful glance. The dream of the faceless man still weighed heavily on him. Was it just a nightmare or was the faceless man real? If so, who was he and what did he want?

"Come on," Demetri said, and led the way into the hills.

The trees and undergrowth quickly closed in around them so that by the time they reached the base of the Bird Boulders the foliage was so thick they could hardly see more than an arm's length in any direction.

"What are we looking for?" Demetri said.

"Your guess is as good as mine. A path, steps, a cave, anything that might be the Forgotten Way."

"It's daunting. This could take hours, days. Let's split up so we can cover more ground. But keep in touch so we don't get lost."

They took separate paths and were quickly out of sight of each other. Ali pushed through the thick undergrowth, insects buzzing and flitting around him. He hailed Demetri a few times and Demetri called back, but thus far neither had found anything of interest to report.

Ali emerged unexpectedly into a field of rose-violet autumn crocus flowers, swaying gently in the breeze. He stood admiring them for a moment, captivated by their beauty. Then he glimpsed a flash of colour and movement out of the corner of his eye.

He crossed to a bank of thick boxwood shrubs and peered into their evergreen foliage. But there was nothing there. Then he had a prickly feeling on the back of his neck, like someone was watching him.

He spun around.

A gemeye was hovering directly in front of him. It clacked its broad beak, its bright jewel-like eyes a myriad of moving colours, its crystalline plumage reflecting the yellow-green hues of the boxwood.

Ali took a tentative step towards it.

With a mere flick of its wings the bird moved a short distance away then halted, hovering again.

He edged closer and it did the same thing.

It seemed to be waiting for him and, even though he knew that was absurd, he had the feeling the gemeye wanted him to follow it. He knew he should call out to Demetri but was afraid the sound of his voice might frighten the bird away. So he decided to follow it and see what would happen.

He approached the luck bird again, and this time it didn't flit straight away but paused, hovering, staring eye to eye with him for a few seconds. Then it flicked its wings and plunged into a dense stand of boxwoods.

Ali took off after it. He pushed his way into the thicket, only to have the ground suddenly fall away beneath him. He dropped straight down, as though through a trapdoor, and his cry for help was left behind as he plummeted into pitch-black darkness.

19. The Forgotten Way

Ali tumbled down, bumping and twisting, faster and faster, out of control. His stomach was in his throat and he couldn't breathe. It would have been exhilarating if it wasn't terrifying. Then he gasped, realising he was not actually falling, but sliding. Like he was sliding down a steep grass bank, except instead of a hill, he was skimming down a rock chute. A watercourse perhaps. So far, the rock was smooth, but he was afraid that if he hit a crag or spur it would split or tear him apart. Either that or he would surely crash in a pile of broken bones at the bottom.

Then the chute began to level out and Ali started to slow, sliding to a crunching halt in a pile of sand and gravel. Everything was pitch black. He clambered shakily to his knees, his heart pounding. He shouted to Demetri for help, but the only reply to come back was the echo of his own voice. He yelled and yelled until he was hoarse, but still there was no reply.

In a panic, he scrambled back into the rock chute, trying to claw his way to the top, but after a few metres it slanted up at such an acute angle that no matter how hard he tried he slid back every time. Finally, after slipping back to the bottom one time too many, he sprawled there, exhausted and miserable, his chest heaving.

Demetri might never find me, he thought. What would happen to Rose if he couldn't get out of here? He would never find Luman or his father. And his dreams would cease to be significant because he would die down here…

"Over my dead body," he said to himself. Then realised how

ridiculous that sounded. Because that was exactly what would happen if he didn't get out of there.

He got back to his hands and knees, and groped around the sandy floor for his belongings. He found his shoulder sack nearby and rummaged through it by touch until he located the tinder pouch and candle. He pulled the makings from the pouch, struck the steel piece across the sharp edge of the flint, casting sparks into the tinder fungus, blowing on it until it caught alight. He then lit the candle from the burning tinder and held it high.

He was in some sort of cave or tunnel that disappeared into almost impenetrable darkness.

He figured he had two choices. Either he could wait and hope that Demetri would find him, or he could explore the cave and hope it might lead him somewhere. Neither option appealed, but he reasoned that the hole he had fallen down was so well hidden by undergrowth and boxwood thicket that Demetri might never find him, so his best option was to search the cave.

He packed his tinder pouch away, slung his sack over his shoulder and moved cautiously into the pitch-black opening of the cave, holding the flickering candle out in front of him. The cave was quite large, the floor relatively flat, scattered with loose sand and gravel that had probably been washed down the rock chute over time. The walls and arched ceiling, however, were honeycombed with dark holes, as though made from some colossal cheese or sea-sponge turned to stone.

Ali shone the candle into a couple of the larger holes, wondering if they might afford him a means of escape. They were big enough to crawl into, about the same diameter as a large barrel, but the air inside them had a sour, ammonia-like smell and he thought better of it.

In contrast, the air in the tunnel was relatively fresh, and Ali hoped that the passage might lead somewhere above ground, so he pressed on. He was thinking about the holes in the walls, deciding that the odour he had smelled was not unlike stale cat pee, when suddenly a scraping noise behind him broke the silence.

He whirled around and held the candle high, straining to

peer into the gloom, but could see nothing. Then the sound came again, like something large moving across the gravel on the floor of the cave.

His mouth went dry and his heart raced. He swapped the candle into his left hand and drew his dagger, holding the blade out in front of him.

As if in response, a hideous snarl sounded from the darkness.

Ali turned and fled deeper into the cave.

The candle flickered wildly, casting grotesque shadows on the stone walls, then it blew out, plunging him into utter darkness. He tripped and fell hard. The breath was knocked out of him, and his candle and dagger flew from his grasp.

Before he could recover himself, another growling snarl issued from somewhere in the dark ahead of him. His blood ran cold in his veins. Whatever was making these sounds, there were now two of them. One ahead of him and one behind.

He groped in panic for his dagger, but halted in disbelief when he saw a faint glimmer of light—barely perceivable, but light nonetheless—coming from one of the holes in the wall. It was so dim that if his candle had been alight, he would surely have missed it.

He dived into the opening without a second thought, only to find himself sliding headlong down another rock chute. It twisted and turned, then he shot out at the bottom and landed face first in a pile of loose sand. His shoulder sack landed beside him. Blinking and spitting grit from his mouth, he stood and looked around. Everything was aglow with a yellow-green light. He was standing on the sandy floor of a vast cavern: a subterranean chamber illuminated by the rock itself. The walls, the ceiling, and even the mighty lances and columns of stone thrusting up from the floor and down from the ceiling, all glowed with inner light.

Ali held his breath, taking in the spectacle of the place, awe-struck by its cathedral-like splendour. On the far side of the cavern, a magnificent waterfall fell crashing from vaulted heights into a broad lake that filled three-quarters of the chamber. The mist it threw up was alive with tiny rainbow sparkles.

At the edge of the lake was a stone pier reaching out into the water. A pair of small rowboats were moored alongside it. Nearby, a dinghy had been pulled onto the beach. People had clearly been here before him. It struck him that he had unwittingly stumbled upon the very thing he had been searching for: the Lost River and the Forgotten Way spoken of by the Wandering Pilgrim.

He ran across the sandy beach and out along the pier, but his excitement was short-lived when over the echoing clamour of the waterfall a menacing snarl came from the beach behind him. He spun around to find a large, brown-scaled lizard-like creature armed with a mouthful of crocodilian teeth glaring at him with huge, bulging eyes.

As he stared in horror, a second creature fell with a *thud* from the chute down which Ali himself had slid only moments before. This one was a different colour, purplish-grey instead of brown, but its teeth were equally menacing. It snarled and lifted its ugly head, large eyes blinking, and charged towards him.

It moved surprisingly fast, but Ali was faster and he leaped into the nearest rowboat moored alongside the pier. Instead of landing in it, though, his feet punched straight through the bottom of the boat's hull, its rotten timbers disintegrating under his weight. He plunged into the cold, clear water of the lake beneath the boat.

He struggled to the surface and swam clear, just as the creature lunged into the boat after him. Its legs, too, went through the bottom of the hull, except its neck and tail fell across the gunwales, wedging it in the sinking craft.

Ali splashed to the shore, hauled himself from the lake, and cast an anxious glance back. The purplish lizard creature had freed itself from the damaged rowboat and was thrashing in the water, trying to clamber back onto the pier. A growl from the beach alerted him that its companion was nearby, and he searched desperately around for some means of escape.

There was little choice. The beach on which he stood was bordered on one side by the lake, and on the other side by the honeycombed rock wall from which he and the creatures had emerged. There had once been stairs carved into the rock face leading to a wide ledge and a dark doorway high above, but the steps had collapsed midway and were now little more than a pile of rubble at the base of the cliff.

In desperation, Ali dashed to the third boat sitting high and dry on the beach. He quickly examined it, and to his relief it was sound, its timbers solid. It was a different design to the rowboats in the water: smaller, flatter and oarless, propelled by tiller action instead. He put his shoulder to the transom and shoved. The boat slid easily forward, its keel cutting a groove on the loose sand as it moved, but after a few feet it *clunked* to a halt and refused to budge.

He swallowed hard, his gaze darting from one lizard creature to other. The brownish one on the beach was occupied with Ali's shoulder-sack, tearing it apart with teeth and claws to get at his remaining food supplies. Its purplish mate had managed to pull itself out of the water and was now stalking back along the pier, its fierce gaze fixed on him.

Ali ran to the front of the boat, linked his hands under the prow, and heaved. The nose lifted easily and he was able to swing the craft sideways, revealing the obstruction to be a small mound of rocks. He grabbed two of the larger ones, kicked the rest aside, and darted back to the stern.

With the obstruction cleared, the boat slid freely again and Ali shoved it scraping across the sand and into the water. As if sensing their prey was about to escape, the beasts charged at him from opposite directions, snarling and gnashing their teeth.

Ali flung a rock at each of them in quick succession. He hit the purplish one on the pier on its nose and it shied away with an angry snarl, but he missed the other one. He turned on his heel and splashed into the water, throwing himself into the bobbing craft. He leaped to the tiller and worked it madly. The slavering beasts plunged into the water after him. Thankfully they were poor swimmers, and Ali reached the current of the Lost River well ahead of them. He let out a huge breath and flopped back as the boat was swept away into the subterranean depths below Mount Simeon.

20. A Cry for Help

The river flowed through a wide, vaulted cavern filled with a fairyland of underground wonders. Islands with intricate sculptures of living rock jutted from the river. Delicate grottos of incredible beauty, lit by luminescent minerals that glowed like coloured lights, were set in the cavern walls. Spouts of water spilled from above and picturesque waterfalls cascaded down natural stone steps into the river.

But thrilled as he was by these wonders, Ali's thoughts were focused on his predicament. He might have escaped the cave creatures back at the beach, but he had lost everything except his silver luck coin, which was miraculously still in his purse. He had no food, no dagger or equipment, and he had no idea where he was or where the river was taking him.

The current propelled the dinghy for hour upon hour, or so it seemed, because without the sun or moon it was impossible for him to measure the passage of time, and the river felt like it went on forever.

Eventually, fatigue and the gentle rocking of the dinghy got the better of him and he drifted off to sleep, only to find himself drawn almost immediately into a dream. A dream that belonged to someone else…

He found himself standing in a cold stone cellar lit only by a feeble oil lamp. He was drawn towards a heavy wooden trapdoor set in the flagstone floor. Someone was calling him. Not the faceless man this time, but someone deep below where he stood.

Ali tugged the trapdoor open to reveal a set of stone steps leading down into darkness. He stood for a moment, contemplating the descent. Then the call came again and it was a desperate cry for help. He shivered, and descended the steps.

The air was rank, damp and unhealthy. Moisture trickled down the walls and slimy, grey moss covered the lower steps. He felt his way along a dark, narrow passage which brought him to a bolted timber door. He unlatched the bolt, yanked the door open and stepped through the doorway. Small, dark shapes scurried chittering out of his way.

It was a dungeon. A place designed for people to suffer. There, staked out on some sort of apparatus in the middle of the room, a naked, emaciated man peered at him. He was alight with a sorcerous, eerie glow that illuminated the cell with a ruddy light and charged the air with the smell of red-hot metal. This was the man who had called for help. This was the man whose dream he had entered.

He recognised him. It came to Ali in a single *knowing*, the way things do in dreams. The man was a Dreamer… He was the Wandering Pilgrim… He was the peculiar sailor… He was Ali's own *father*. He was all these men, they were one and the same.

But the importance, the significance of this, was overwhelmed by the man's terrible pain and fatigue. Ali rushed to him and threw his arms around his father. Both were weeping and even in the dream he could taste the salt of their mingled tears.

His father tried to speak, but all that came out of his mouth was a feeble croak. Yet their minds were connected in a way that Ali could hear or see or feel his father's thoughts. *Must stop Savich. End the blood magic. You are our last hope, my son.* But his message was weak and fading rapidly.

It was then that Ali realised how much effort it was costing his father to reach out to him. The toll on the man was frightful, for this place was more than a physical prison. A dark power held his father in thrall, *blood magic* he called it, suppressing his ability to dream.

Ali instinctively took the burden, took control of the dream. The shift was subtle, almost seamless, but enough to allow his father to collapse back and let go of the agony that racked him to his core.

Suddenly Ali was jerked awake, leaving the dream unfinished. Like a curtain come down prematurely on a theatre performance. He tried to force the dream to go on, but it was no use, it was gone. And with it, so too his father…

What had woken him?

He sat up. The boat was racing along at a cracking pace. In the near distance, an ominous rumble echoed in the chamber. The river tossed the boat around a bend, making it buck and dip in the swell. Ali grabbed the tiller and braced himself. Water sloshed over the sides and spray soaked him.

Ahead, a colossal stone wall reared up from a maelstrom of foam and spray, marking the end of both the cavern and the river.

A deafening roar filled the chamber.

The dinghy was hurtling straight for the centre of the tumult. Ali leaned on the tiller, trying to turn the boat, but it did not respond. Waves surged over the sides, swamping the little craft. He cast about for a way out. Through the spray he thought he saw some manmade stonework near the right-hand bank. Perhaps a ledge or steps against the wall where the water looked calmer.

Then he was flung sideways and the scene was gone. The boat was no longer going straight but spinning, and Ali realised he was being sucked into a whirlpool. The water in the boat was nearly level with the gunwales and it was surely sinking. He had no choice but to abandon it. He lurched to his feet, pulled off his cloak, tossed it aside, and leaped into the river.

The current grabbed him and sucked him into its swirling spiral.

Ali rose spluttering to the surface and squinted through the spray, trying to orient himself in the massive chamber. The rock wall at the end whizzed past and he realised that any moment the whirlpool was going to spin him as close to the right-hand bank as he would ever be.

With every bit of strength and determination he could summon he launched himself for the bank, battling the relentless pull of the current. His feet churned and his arms thrashed but he barely seemed to be moving. The harder he tried, the more the gushing torrent sapped his energy.

He told himself to stay calm and focused all his concentration on one stroke at a time—*stroke…stroke…stroke*—until gradually, hand over hand, he inched away from the centre of the vortex.

Finally, after what felt like an eternity, his hand struck stone. He blinked water from his eyes. He was bobbing in comparatively still waters eddying along the stone wall at the river's edge. Nearby, a set of steps led up and out of the water.

Trembling with utter fatigue, Ali dragged himself along the wall to the steps and used every last vestige of energy to haul himself from the river. He collapsed onto the steps, sodden and exhausted, his hair plastered to his face, and laid there for a long time until his breathing gradually returned to normal and he recovered some strength.

He sat up and looked around. There was a ledge above him cut into the rock along the wall of the cavern. Below in the swirling maelstrom, there was no sign of his boat.

His vest, shirt and trousers were sodden, so he peeled them off and wrung them out, feeling a pang of regret when he found his purse missing. The luck coin given to him by the peculiar sailor—by his *father*—was gone. Taken by the whirlpool.

He dressed again and stumbled along the ledge, trusting this truly was the Forgotten Way that would lead him to Luman. Then he pulled a wry face, thinking that if this was the usual way of reaching the path, he was not surprised people had forgotten about it. He steadied himself against the wall, the stone underfoot slippery with spray, and came to another flight of steep stairs that led through an archway carved in the rock. He took one final look back into the chamber, at the turbulent maelstrom below, and started up the steps.

The passage was lit by seams of luminous agate in the rock walls. Ali trudged laboriously up one step after another, climbing in an interminable spiral. His legs ached and cramped, but he pushed through the pain, because everything hung on finding Luman. Both his mother and his father—in his various guises—had told him so. For without Luman's help Ali knew he had no way of finding and freeing either Rose or his father, let alone learning how to control his dreams.

After a while the glowing stone that lighted the path dwindled, until once again he was plunged into total darkness, forced to feel his way up the stairs on hands and knees.

And still the passage went on.

It wasn't until the passage started to get warmer that he realised he was about to emerge into the open air for the first time since he had followed the luck bird and fallen down the shaft near the Bird Boulders. That made him think of Demetri and he wondered what had become of his friend, hoping he was all right.

A glimmer of light turned into a dazzling shaft of brilliance as he clambered up the last few sand-covered steps and emerged into the fierce heat of Bādiyah Ash-Shām. He squinted, shielding his watering eyes with his hands, and stared across the vast, arid landscape.

What was he to do? The desert was sun-baked sand, gravel and rock in every direction, with barely a tuft of dry grass or stunted bush in sight.

Common sense told him to stay where he was. Down below there was water, plenty of water. And there was shelter from the blazing sun. There was no food, of course. But he could base himself here and make forays into the desert. Perhaps find or catch something to eat: a hamster—cute though they might be—or some other rodent, or bird, or even a wild cat or ass. He would eat a snake if it came down to it. But how he would catch, kill and prepare these things? He had lost his dagger and tinder pouch, and he didn't have any hunting skills except for his ability to throw stones and rocks.

But he would not find Luman if he stayed here.

A bird flew overhead, little more than a dark speck against a cloudless, pale-blue sky, flying eastwards. He ducked, at first fearing it might be a carrion crow scouting for him. But it ignored him and flew on. Thinking about it, he reckoned that birds need water, so maybe that was the way to head. Nodding to himself, he decided to shelter here until sundown and then set off into the desert in the cool of night in search of Luman.

He would follow the bird.

21. The Bādiyah Ash-Shām

The next day, as the first rays of dawn lit the eastern horizon, Ali scrabbled wearily to the top of a rocky ridge to survey the way ahead. He had trekked all night without food or water and he wondered, not for the first time, if he should turn back.

His desire, his *need,* to find Luman, however, gave him no choice.

Ahead, the thin morning light revealed a sea of flat, stony ground the colour of dried carrots, with the occasional bank of sand dunes, that stretched forever. He sighed and chided himself for abandoning his shoulder-sack to the cave creatures, because he feared that without any supplies the desert would quickly claim and desiccate him.

He half-slid down the ridge and pressed on, the rising sun already hot on his face. Within the hour it was blazing with fiery intensity. He stopped briefly, sweat running down his back and chest, to pull his faded blue vest over his head for protection, and kept moving forward, driven by thoughts of Rose and his father. Driven by the understanding that the only way he could help them, the only way he could help himself, was to keep going until he found Luman.

Underfoot, the gritty sand crunched beneath his calloused feet, a flat monotonous landscape virtually devoid of life, broken only by sand dunes, rocky sandstone outcrops and occasional tufts of desiccated saltwort tussock grass. He had been warned and now he knew the truth of it: few people aside from the nomadic Bedouin ever survived the Bādiyah Ash-Shām.

Then, as if in an attempt to disprove the desert's reputation, a small sand-coloured jerboa darted on long, thin legs out of a clump of saltbush.

His heart leaped. If he was lucky, here was food.

He dashed after it, but the little animal was faster than him and any hope of catching it quickly faded. It darted across a stony flat area, then it slid to an inexplicable halt and froze, trembling.

For a moment Ali was elated, but just when he was about to pounce, he too froze.

A deadly yellow-brown mottled viper shot out of the sand, reared up and struck lightning fast. Its mouth opened impossibly wide and snapped shut over the jerboa, the bite driving its long fangs and venom deep into the hapless rodent's flesh. The snake held the creature until its quivering and twitching ceased, then devoured it, swallowing it whole.

Ali stood stock-still, watching the viper and studying the surface of the desert around him. The reptile was virtually the same colour as the sand, almost invisible unless you looked hard. It moved away in a side-winder pattern, leaving tell-tale parallel lines across the ground, before wriggling back beneath the sand to digest its meal.

There were similar marks on the sand all around him. Ali bent and picked up a pebble, bowling it underarm across the ground. The blood ran from his face when three more vipers shot to the surface and tried to bite the stone. They hissed angrily, the rough scales along their length making a rasping sound as they writhed and twisted in frustration. He gulped. He was surrounded by snakes.

Holding his breath, Ali pushed his sweaty hair off his face and backed carefully out the way he had come.

It had been a close call, unnecessarily close, because Demetri had warned him about snakes and he should have been more careful. With that thought in mind, he gave the area a wide berth and resumed his thankless search, scanning the ground ahead for threats as he walked.

By mid-morning he was still trudging exhausted, up and down one dune after another, the loose sand making every step an effort. He paused, wiped stinging sweat from his eyes, and squinted into the bright sky. A bird was circling overhead, but where once it might have given him hope, now he assumed it might be a crow, or if not, a vulture to pick his bones.

Ali stood there exhausted, swaying like a sapling in a breeze, his legs weary and aching, his thoughts swimming. A little voice in his head tried to persuade him to lie down, reasoning that if he allowed himself to rest, to sleep, he could dream his way out of his predicament. But another more compelling voice that sometimes sounded like Rose, and other times like his mother, or the peculiar sailor or the Wandering Pilgrim, told him not to give up.

He shuffled onwards, calling on every last skerrick of strength until finally, halfway up a dune, he stumbled and collapsed, utterly exhausted. But even as he lay there with his face in the sand the small voice in his head urged him forward, urged him to find Luman.

Just a little bit further, it said.

He pushed himself back to his hands and knees and crawled forward, spitting hot, gritty sand from his parched mouth. He reached the top of the dune and peered over the other side.

His eyes bulged.

In the hollow between himself and the crest of the next dune lay what appeared to be a full waterskin.

He let out a hoarse laugh, only to fall silent, a sinking feeling in his gut as the realisation struck him that he must be hallucinating. He had always imagined a mirage to be a wraith-like, insubstantial thing, but this delusion was as tangible and well defined as the real thing.

He stared longingly at the waterskin, unable to ignore its allure, even though he knew it must be a figment of his fevered imagination. In the end, he could stand it no longer and he crawled and half tumbled down the sandy slope, and fell upon it.

The waterskin *felt* real. He got to his knees and raised it. It wobbled like a jellyfish, full and bloated. But before he could remove the stopper and try to drink from this all-too-real hallucination, a hideous, tortured cry pulled him up short.

He looked around, bewildered. He gazed at the waterskin and then at the ground around him. For the first time he noticed a trail of footprints in the sand leading away from where he was kneeling. They led up and over the next dune. He stood shakily, slung the waterskin over his shoulder, and cautiously followed the tracks.

The footprints led down the other side of the dune into a broad orange-brown sand flat crossed with revealing viper tracks. In the middle of the area a frail-looking, white-haired old woman stood frozen in terror.

Her way was blocked on three sides by hissing and rasping snakes. As she shuffled towards the largest one, it reared up at her approach, as long as Ali's arm and as thick as his wrist, its pointed fangs bared.

"Stop," Ali said, his voice a dry croak in his parched throat.

"Help us," the woman cried in a surprisingly strong voice, considering her feeble, wizened appearance. "Help us. We are surrounded." But she continued to move away from him into obvious danger.

Ali dropped the waterskin and staggered to the old woman's aid, warily negotiating a safe path between where he guessed vipers were buried. When he reached her, he took hold of the old woman's hand and pulled her away.

"What are you doing?" she said in a fearful voice.

"Trying to rescue you," he croaked, easing her back away from the vipers. "Are you crazy? You're walking straight into them." He was about to chastise her more, but fell silent when she turned to face him.

She was blind, her eyes glassy, unseeing milky-white orbs.

"I'm sorry. I mean…"

"Our water, we've lost our water," the old woman said.

"We?" Ali asked. "Is there someone else?"

"Thief!" the woman screeched, ignoring his question. "It's *our* water. We'll die without our water."

"Your water is over there where I dropped it," he said.

"Aye, take it then, scoundrel. Save yourself. What use is a blind old hermit woman to anyone? Aye, we'll die anyway so don't bother about us. Go on, take our water and be on your way."

Ali ignored her ranting and guided her safely from the sand viper area, back to where he had dropped the waterskin. The old woman's tirade stopped only when Ali placed the nozzle of the waterskin to her lips. She snatched it from him and took a deep draught, smacking her lips before drinking again.

When finally she finished and handed the skin to Ali, he took small, reviving sips. It was the sweetest water he had ever tasted. When he was done, he stoppered the nozzle and slung the strap of the waterskin over the old woman's shoulder.

"What's this?" she said in mock appreciation.

"Your waterskin."

"Aye, of course it's our waterskin. Does that mean you are not abandoning us?" And she gave a laugh that sounded like the cackle of a hen.

"Why would I abandon you?" he asked. "We can help each other if we stick together."

"We suppose that means you want us to share our water with you." Again, the strength of her voice surprised him. "Aye, we know, we know, we should be thankful you did not kill us for our water."

His eyes bulged. "Kill you?"

"It would have done you no good even if you had killed us. You would still have died. Aye, without our help the Bādiyah Ash-Shām will still be your end. And we can't have that, so now we suppose we'll have to take you back to our home."

"Your *home*?"

"Aye, our home. It's either that or leave you here to perish." She cackled again in a way that made him uneasy.

She took hold of his arm. "Head towards the north-east and keep your eyes open for a large rocky outcrop with a bird circling above it."

Ali wearily led her across the hot sand and wondered if he was sane to be going along with her. Was it possible she had a home here in the desert? Might she be able to help him to find Luman? Or was she completely crazy and would they both die here in the desert?

When they finally reached the massive sandstone outcrop, he was near collapse, his breath shallow, his feet blistered and numb, his legs trembling.

The old woman let go of his arm and felt her way along the face of the rocks. Then she beckoned him to follow and squeezed her way between two monolithic boulders. He followed and she deftly wended her way through a maze of rocks and massive standing stones until they stepped into a sandy clearing.

Before them stood the dark, gaping mouth of a cave.

There was a whispering flutter above them and a stocky luck bird, sun glinting off its wings in iridescent rainbow spears, descended into the clearing to alight gently on the old woman's shoulder.

Then she took Ali's hand in hers and led him into the cave.

22. The Gemeye Chamber

"This is our home," the old woman said.

She had led him, stumbling with fatigue, down through a warren of pitch-black passages and caves, to an innermost chamber deep below the desert.

Ali gazed around the interior of the cave.

The muddy red light from the coals in a fire-pit revealed a crude timber table, a chair, shelves made of planks laid across stakes driven into the wall, and a sleeping pallet on the floor.

She led him to the pallet, the stout gemeye perched on her shoulder all the while, and eased him onto a bed of dried brush where he collapsed, his last skerrick of energy gone. His head thumped, his muscles ached, and his face, neck and arms were burned red raw, hot and blistered.

The old woman went to one of the shelves and returned to squat beside him. She poured a spoonful of syrup from a clay bottle and dribbled it into his mouth. It was both sweet and peppery, and it warmed his insides as it went down.

"It will help to ease your pain, help you sleep and heal," she said.

She did not spill a drop, he realised, and he wondered if she was truly blind.

"You can call us 'Sister'," she said. "What are you called and what are you doing alone in the desert?"

"Ali," he said, his voice rasping. "My name is Ali. I am searching for Luman."

"Aye, many have come to the desert seeking Luman—their

bleached bones protrude from Bādiyah Ash-Shām's timeless sands."

"I must find Luman," he said, trying to sit. But the effort made him dizzy and nauseate and he dropped back onto the brush.

"Aye. You won't be going anywhere until you have healed and regained your strength. You almost died. Had you not found us the Bādiyah Ash-Shām would have claimed you too."

"Luman," he mumbled, his head awhirl.

"You are sunburned, dehydrated and starving," she said. "You could not have survived much longer without water and yet you still returned our waterskin. Why…?"

He bit his lip and gave a weak shrug.

"Aye," she continued. "You saved us from the sand vipers and returned our waterskin when many would have abandoned us and kept the water for themselves." This time it was a statement.

"We could've sh…a…r…ed…" he said distantly as exhaustion overcame him and he slipped into unconsciousness.

He drifted in and out of a delirium-filled sleep for what seemed like days, remembering little that made any sense. When the fugue finally broke, he found Sister sitting over him, mopping his brow, dripping a salty-sweet nectar into his mouth.

The fog eventually left his head, but his body took longer to mend. Sister nursed him, fed him warm *aşure*—a sweet, thick porridge made of wheat, dried fruit and nuts—which she spooned gently between his parched, cracked lips, and she massaged salve into his blistered feet, and soothing balm into his sunburned skin.

Thanks to her ministrations, he recovered slowly but steadily from his ordeal.

She moved easily around the cave, as nimble as a sighted person, the ever-present luck bird perched three toes pointed forward, one toe pointed backward on her shoulder. Ali began to believe she was indefatigable, until one morning she was inexplicably struck down. One minute she was standing, bent over the steaming contents of a cooking pot on the fire-pit, and the next minute she screamed in pain and tumbled onto her back, racked by convulsions. She clutched her head with rigid fingers, white froth bubbling from her lips, spasms twisting her aged frame.

The luck bird on her shoulder lurched into the air, opened its long, wide beak, and let out a keening wail.

Ali jumped up and rushed to her aid, but didn't know what to do. He turned her on her side, gently placed a cushion of dried grass under her head, and held her to try to stop her injuring herself as one painful spasm after another made her buck and writhe in agony.

It lasted a minute or more, then it was gone. When the final seizure passed, and Sister's breathing returned to normal, he asked what was wrong, but she brushed his concern aside.

"Just a twinge," she said.

But they both knew it was more than that. Something was wrong.

"I have to leave soon," he told her that night. "Now that my strength is returning, I have to try to find Luman. But I am worried about you. Will you be all right?"

She nodded, but he did not really believe her.

"Is there anything I can do for you before I leave?" he asked. "Anything I can do to repay your help and kindness?"

She leaned slightly towards the luck bird perched on her shoulder and its eyes blazed, then she clasped Ali's hand and gave it a squeeze. "Aye. Before you go, we would have you do something for us." Sister took some empty waterskins from their pegs on the wall and held them out to him. "We would have you take these down to the Lost River and fill them for us."

He accepted them from her. "It's the least I can do. You saved my life. How do I find my way?"

She raised her arm and the gemeye on her shoulder hopped onto her outstretched hand. It clacked its kingfisher-like beak, and watched him for a moment, embers lighting its eyes.

"Aye," she said. "You can follow us."

She took a pinch of powder from one of the many canisters on her shelves and sprinkled it over the bird, wiping the fine particles across the bird's wings so that they shimmered with a faint luminescence.

Then the gemeye launched itself into the air, hovered briefly to make sure Ali understood, before flicking its crystalline wings and plunging into the darkness at the rear of the cave.

He jogged after the gemeye, knowing that he was meant to follow it but wondering how he could keep it in sight. Then he saw that the gemeye was leaving him a trail, a faint comet-like glow hanging in the darkness behind the bird, a phosphorescent wake that enabled him to follow it.

The bird flew swiftly through the rocky maze of tunnels that crisscrossed the subterranean depths beneath the cave, spiralling ever deeper through the unmapped passages from which one might never emerge without a guide.

In places Ali had to run to keep up, unable to even pause to catch his breath, for if he lagged too far behind the gemeye's guiding trail began to fade from sight. Without that he would be lost, alone in the dark.

A chill ran down his spine. The lizard creatures from his previous cave experience were still vivid in his memory, and he shuddered at the thought of what else might be lurking here in the dark. For a moment, he wondered if Sister had sent him down here with some sort of malign intent. But he dismissed the thought as absurd, ducking and turning in pursuit of the gemeye, knowing in his heart that he could trust the old woman.

As if in confirmation, there was suddenly light ahead and the sound of running water. He dashed eagerly forward, his heart racing, and burst into a cavern to find the Lost River stretching before him.

As on the previous occasion when he had stumbled upon the Forgotten Way and first seen the underground river, the cavern through which it ran was illuminated by the rock itself. But this time there was a difference. This cavern was swarming with living creatures. Gemeyes young and old, thousands of birds filled the chamber.

It was widely thought that gemeyes were rare creatures. They were ancient, as old as the land, but where once, according to legend, they had flocked in great profusion, their number was now assumed to be so small that people thought it good luck to even catch a glimpse of one.

Yet here, in this cavern deep beneath the most inhospitable desert in the land, they swarmed in abundance: perched in crevasses and on ledges, standing where they had been feeding en masse on the bushy white moss-like growth that covered the river banks, hovering in the air.

Ali blinked. He could not believe what he was seeing. There were more luck birds here than he had ever imagined existed in the entire world. But they were eerily silent and still—not a single chirp, squawk or movement escaped from them.

Until, as one, each and every gemeye simultaneously turned to look at him.

23. Communion and Revelation

Ali gulped.

Every faceted eye held him, probing. His skin prickled and crawled. He could *feel* the gemeyes' scrutiny, felt naked and exposed beneath their gaze.

Then they were *inside* him, peeling away the onion-like layers of his very being. His thoughts, memories, desires, regrets; all were incised and inspected, evaluated.

He could feel the birds weighing his essence, not as observers, but as participants, as though they were actually part of him and had experienced the events of his life. Then the sense of probing gently ebbed, although their friendly presence remained, like a warm glow within him.

As one, the birds in the cavern lifted into the air and flocked around him, a vast cloud, hovering, pressing towards him. One landed on his head, others on his shoulders. He stretched his arms wide and they perched there, bringing with them a new sensation.

They opened *their* minds to him.

A vast wave of love and compassion swept over him, exhilarating, overwhelming. He almost staggered under its intensity. There was a sense of welcome, of kinship. Then he was inside their thoughts, *part* of them, experiencing *their* memories, their feelings. Becoming part of their connectedness and their oneness. For even though they were all individuals, the gemeyes were also somehow joined together so that they seemed to have a single mind.

What was even more amazing was that *he* had joined with them as their consciousness engulfed him. He saw himself through their eyes from hundreds of different positions and angles, standing with his arms wide like a scarecrow. He could smell himself, taste his musky odour, new amongst the familiar scents of the cave. He saw everything the gemeyes saw, felt what they felt, heard all that they heard, remembered their memories:

Freedom…

He found himself soaring through the air, gliding on thermal currents over the desert, feeling the breeze on his face, ruffling his hair. He saw familiar places: the Korykos waterfront, the İskenderūn bazaar. He saw scenes from faraway places: the minarets of Amasya, the Ayasofya of Constantinople.

Connected…

He communed with others who had visited this underground bird sanctuary in times past. Young men and women from across the ages, dreamers like himself come in search of guidance. All were now long gone, but they were still alive in the gemeyes' communal memory. He recognised them as kin, and recognised the goodness in their hearts.

Love…

Hope…

He saw himself in the gemeyes' memories and realised they had been watching him for some time. He saw himself talking to the peculiar sailor in Korykos before he knew the man was his father. Knew they had purposely protected him on the wall of the İskenderūn slave market and lured him into the forest above the Lost River. They had watched him cross the desert and return the old woman's waterskin. He perceived that in him they saw hope for the land, hope for the people and hope for themselves.

Awareness…

They shared an ancient truth. That the world was an entity, a living, sensing organism. Tengri or whatever faith-name you wanted to call him/her was the creator of life, of the universe. Mother and father, sanctuary to all living things.

But with that knowledge came the understanding she was ailing. He felt her pain, her cry for help, and knew that life as he knew it was in great peril.

Sadness...

Fear...

He saw men hunting and trapping gemeyes, caging them. Ruthless, greedy men with little respect for anyone or anything. Except perhaps for the evil one they served, but even then, Ali knew it was more fear than respect that these men felt for their master. He saw the men deliver the caged gemeyes to a puffy-faced, sunken-eyed bald man who paid them in opium and large sums of gold coins.

Ali felt the trapped birds' terror and despair, as though it was he *himself* who was ensnared, and he began to tremble. Not the least because he recognised their paymaster as the very same leering, bald-headed man with black pits for eyes who haunted his nightmares.

And now he had a name for the faceless nightmare-man. The gemeyes knew him. It was *Savich.*

Despair...

Revulsion...

Then, the communal gemeye mind prepared Ali gently and with great compassion for a further shock. Even so, when the memory was revealed to him, his knees went weak.

Because the remembrance was of Rose, the slave girl, locked and weeping in a windowless room. He saw the image through the eyes of a gemeye imprisoned in a cage held high by Savich as he stood over her, gloating. It came to Ali in a gemeye memory that Savich was purposely showing Rose's situation to the bird so that it could see her peril, her palpable fear. So that *all* the gemeyes and those connected to them would know of the girl's plight, feel her terror.

After that Ali was shown another memory, this one of his friend Demetri, his wrists and ankles bound, being savagely beaten by thugs with clubs. Ali could hear the men's grunts, Demetri's cries of pain. He saw it all from the perspective of a gemeye held aloft in a cage by Savich.

Then Ali saw his *father*—naked and staked on a torture rack in a deep dungeon. Just as he had seen in his dream in the boat on the river, except this time Savich was also in the picture. The puffy-faced, hairless man was laughing as he watched a torturer yank out his father's finger and toenails with iron pliers.

Tears streamed down Ali's cheeks. The birds, too, were weeping in their own way.

The gemeyes could not only see his father's plight, but they could also *feel* his suffering. Because in his youth his father, like Ali himself was now doing, had come to this very place and communed with the gemeyes.

Ali not only saw the pain in his father's sad, gentle brown eyes, but actually felt the rip and tear, the agony as each nail was torn from his fingers. What's more, he heard and felt his father's thoughts, suddenly understanding there was much more at play here than he could ever have guessed.

And he now knew for certain that Savich was behind everything, was responsible for the pain and suffering of his friends and his father, his mother's murder, and his own abduction and internment with Fedar. The pretender to the throne had perpetrated all these crimes because he wanted to control Ali's dreams.

Savich wanted power and revenge and was willing to do anything, pay any price, to get them.

With great pain and sorrow, the gemeyes summoned another memory. Ali saw a wire cage in which half a dozen gemeyes were confined. Saw Savich open the cage and reach his hand inside. Felt him grab hold and remove a gemeye, one of his new brethren. The cage door slammed shut, there was a blade, the slash of cold steel, and a gout of bright red blood.

Our life-blood.

In horror, Ali watched the hideous bald head, its thick-lipped mouth open, drinking the gemeye blood, using it to amplify his dark powers. Blood magic. To attack all that stood in his path.

Loss…

Grief…

Overwhelming, tragic despair swept through the gemeye flock, through Ali. With the loss of that one life an integral part of them was gone, extinguished.

Sadness…

Ali saw a young woman locked in a bare room, a mother with a baby. She was singing softly, adoringly to the infant, rocking it gently in her arms, tears running down her face. He recognised himself and his mother and he felt her love for him, her fear and grief because she knew she was going to lose him, more concerned for him than herself.

Dread…

Finally, the birds showed him one last memory. Ali found himself back in the old hermit woman's cave beneath the desert, perched on her shoulder while she went about her business of nursing him back to health after his near-fatal trek across the desert.

He heard her cry in distress, saw her crumple to the cave floor. He felt shards of evil twisting in her head, watched helplessly while she writhed in agony, and realised Savich was using the gemeye blood to direct his black powers at her to sap her vital energy. To neutralise her power and deplete her very soul.

For this old woman was all that stood in the way of Savich's quest for power. No mere blind old hermit woman was she, because the gemeyes revealed she was in fact *Luman*.

Luman, who had existed since the beginning of time. Luman, who had had many faces but one essence, one memory. Luman, who was the guardian of the people, of the land, the bridge between man and nature.

Then she herself was inside him with the birds, a part of them, in constant communion. Physically blind, but able to see all that the birds could see.

She *was* Luman, Tengri's servant, God's servant, by whatever name or faith one held.

And she was *dying*.

With the aid of gemeye blood and dark dreaming, Savich was perverting and controlling Ali's own father's dreams to attack and kill her.

24. Luman

Ali emerged from the catacombs to find Luman waiting for him, the ever-present gemeye perched atop her shoulder acting, among other things, as her eyes. The old woman embraced Ali lovingly, whispering congratulations in a voice hoarse with emotion.

"Master," he said, dropping to his knees, "what do you wish of me?"

"We wish you to stand. Enough of this grovelling. Call us Sister as you did before. We have not changed."

"I can't believe you are Luman," he said.

"Aye." She turned and shuffled to the fire-pit to poke at the coals.

He followed her, shaking his head with incredulity. "The legends tell us Luman is a man."

"Luman has been many men and many women," she said. Then she grimaced suddenly, reaching out to grasp his shoulder to steady herself.

In the light from the fire she looked haggard and exhausted. Now he could feel her pain.

She gave a grim nod. "Luman might be immortal but we are not. We are very, very old. But even so, we fear our time to join with Tengri is coming sooner than we expected."

A silence fell between them. Then Ali's stomach growled, and they both laughed.

"You need to eat," she said, moving across to the fireplace. "You must be famished, you have been gone almost two days..."

He gasped. "Two days!"

She served him a triangle of flatbread and a bowl of hot, sweet *aşure*. "You would have been gone even longer had it not been necessary for us to cut short your communion."

"You summoned me back?"

She stroked his face. "Savich's assaults are getting stronger and coming more frequently. To be frank, we don't know how much longer we can withstand them."

"But you are Luman."

"Aye. But Savich's powers are strong, enhanced with gemeye blood, and your own father's corrupted dreams."

"My father is resisting him. I felt it."

"Aye. Your father is doing his best to resist, fighting the good fight, but Savich has him ensorcelled. Even as our strength fails, so does your father's. Savich's attacks on us are also draining for your father, perhaps even killing him."

"Can you stop Savich?"

"Not us, Ali. It is *you* who must stop him."

"*Me*?" he said in a disbelieving voice, doubting her, doubting himself.

"Aye. You said you were seeking your destiny, seeking a purpose to your dreams. This is it. This is the very reason you dream: to pit yourself against the evil that seeks to corrupt God's good work."

"But I thought you would…"

"We have tried," she said with a pained expression. "But Savich's attacks have weakened us."

Ali went pale and swallowed. "Why me?"

She touched his cheek. "You have the qualities and the power. The blood of many generations of Dream Weavers courses through your veins."

He backed away. "My dreams are uncontrollable, what you ask is impossible."

"You were lost to us, Ali, but now you are found. If you can learn to guide your dreams from your heart, you can defeat Savich. You are our last hope, the last hope we have of overcoming his evil blood magic."

"You think I can just dream him away?"

"Of course not," she said. "The ability to Dream is granted to us by sacred Tengri, by God, to help keep the balance between good and evil. You cannot consciously direct your dreams. They have to be directed by your essence. By your heart and soul, not by your mind."

He frowned. "What about Davud? He directed his dreams with his mind."

"Dreams come briefly to some, people with remnants of the Blood. Most simply believe they are experiencing prophetic dreams. Davud, however, learned otherwise and was able to control his dreams for a brief time. But it matters not, for the dreams have now left him."

"What about my dreams? I used them for revenge."

"Wild dreaming, Ali. Unfortunately, it happens sometimes during the onset of dreaming. Because you were on your own, without proper guidance, your dreams were misguidedly trying to protect you."

He held his head in his hands. "I killed a fisherman."

"Not you, dear boy. It was not your fault. You did not choose to do this deed. It was wild dreaming."

"Exactly! My dreams are uncontrollable."

"Evil is always at work in the world, Ali," she said in a soothing tone. "This is why we need a Dream Weaver. And now we need a new one. Someone who has the right qualities, the ability to maintain the balance between good and evil. You can be that one."

"No, not me," he said, alarmed.

"We have seen the power within you. When you face Savich and observe the dark forces that drive him, then you will know what to do."

Ali picked at his food. "Why is Savich doing this, Sister?"

She shrugged. "Jealousy, revenge. He is a cruel, sadistic man. But most of all he wants power, he wants to rule. When Savich was a young man, he schemed to become Sultan. But his father, Bayezid, knew what he was like, that he was somehow broken inside, corrupted and evil, so he had no intention of making Savich his heir."

She shuffled to the chair and eased herself gently onto it. "The trouble began when Savich tried to poison all his brothers in an attempt to gain the throne."

Ali raised his eyebrows. "All his brothers. How?"

"He bribed and coerced the palace kitchen staff with magic. Sultan Bayezid had eight other sons to wives and consorts in his harem. Savich arranged for poisoned food and drink to be served to them all in one fell swoop. Had he been successful, he would have been the only living heir."

"How was his plan foiled?"

"It was the Sultan's Dream Weaver, Erkan, your father. He discovered the plot and dreamed the plot would fail. Until then we don't think Savich really understood the power of dreams."

"What happened to Savich?" Ali asked. "Was he banished?"

Luman shook her head. "Bayezid flew into a rage, he wanted Savich put to death. He ordered the palace guard to strangle him. But in spite of his treachery, Savich still had 'friends' in the Sultan's court at Edirne. They helped him escape to Constantinople where he vanished. Some said he was in Serbia, others said Greece."

Ali scratched his head. "Until recently I had never heard of Savich. He is not mentioned when people speak of Bayezid's sons."

"It was forbidden to speak of him. Most thought him dead. Bayezid sent out secret assassins to locate and kill him, but they either failed to find him or never returned. Savich had vanished completely, even managing to cloak himself from us. Neither me, nor the luck birds, nor Erkan could locate him anywhere. And all the while he was hidden, he was learning dark arts from necromancers and sorcerers, and planning his revenge. The first we knew of him again was when he kidnapped Erkan's young wife and infant son."

"Me and my mother," Ali said, nodding.

"Aye. He killed your mother and you were lost to us for years until you started dreaming. We sensed your power and your father went in search of you."

"I was in Korykos with Fedar."

"Who was in Savich's employ. All these years Savich has been plotting to get even. He has bided his time, employing shadowy forces and learning arcane arts. Now he is strong and without a new Dream Weaver to stand against him, all the world might succumb to his evil. Tengri the Heavenly Father himself is at risk."

Ali squatted by the fire and finished his food in silence, pondering the importance of the old woman's words. He remembered the fear, the revulsion, and the utter desolation he had felt when the gemeyes showed him their memories of Savich.

The puffy face, sunken eyes. The blood…

This was the man, the *beast*, responsible for killing Ali's mother; for his father's incarceration, torment and torture. The man responsible for him, Ali, being orphaned into a life of begging and theft, robbing him of his chance for a normal family. The man responsible for enslaving Rose, the girl he loved; and for beating and torturing his friend Demetri.

Ali felt like he would explode with fury. Either that or weep. Cold rage coursed through his veins, blood pounded in his ears. He wanted vengeance. But these personal things, horrendous and painful as they were, were peripheral to the dangers and terrors Savich was planning to unleash.

Now it fell to him to face Savich. *His* destiny to try and thwart the would-be usurper. It was an impossible task. Others stronger than him had tried and failed. What could *he*, Ali, do? He shivered, fear clutching his heart in a tight grip.

He looked up from his now empty bowl. "It was my hope that my destiny lay in being reunited with my father and making my own way in the world. I…I thought it would be up to others to stop Savich. I don't know what to do, if I can do this. What you are asking of me seems hopeless, but I know I have to try."

"We will not deny there will be great danger, but we would not ask if you had no hope."

"What will happen if I fail?" Ali asked.

"If Savich reaches Amasya and weds the Lady Ashye, Sultan Mehmed will be lost. The scales will be tipped. The empire will fall and Savich will become the despot we fear."

"And if I am successful?"

"Sultan Mehmed will prevail; he will defeat his brothers and balance will be restored."

Ali's brow furrowed. "What about you, Sister? What about my father?"

"When you have defeated Savich, we counsel you to make your way to Amasya and seek one called Kirisci, a sometime resident of the Beyler Palace. Look for him in the maze."

Ali tilted his head. "Why? Who is he?"

She waggled her finger at him. "Because we said so. He will be of help to you."

Ali frowned. "In the maze?"

"Aye. You will find him there in the rose garden. Here"—Luman dug within the folds of her robe—"you will need this." She handed him a shiny object hanging from a plaited grass thong.

"A luck coin," he said, surprised. "I lost one like this in the whirlpool where the Forgotten River is sucked down beneath the desert."

"Aye, and we found it in the river for you. It is the same one you lost. There is only one coin like this. It was your father's, and now it is yours."

He took the coin, fingering its surface, tracing the familiar maze-like pattern. He opened the loop of the thong and hung it around his neck.

"Now you need rest," she said. "For tomorrow you must make haste for Afyonkarahisar."

"The Black Opium Castle?" He shivered. "Why there?"

Luman took hold of his hand. "You are right to fear that place. It is a seat of ancient power. Dark power. It is where Savich now resides."

25. The Black Citadel

It was around midday when Ali and Luman emerged from her underground home beneath the Bādiyah Ash-Shām. He raised his hand to shield his eyes from the glare of the blazing sun and stared towards the north-west, towards Afyonkarahisar.

"Isn't there any way you or my father can help me?" he asked, a nervous fluttering in his stomach.

Luman shook her head regretfully. "I am too weak, Ali. Erkan is ensorcelled by Savich. We are helpless."

He rubbed the back of his neck. "Can no one else help? What of the other dreamers you mentioned?"

"None have endured. You alone have exhibited the right qualities."

A spasm of pain made her stiffen and grit her teeth.

Ali took hold of her hand. "What will become of you, Sister?"

She squeezed his hand gently. "Time is short. The sooner you get to Afyonkarahisar, the better."

"How am I to get there?"

Luman chuckled. "Fly of course. Aye. How else?"

She let go of his hand and cast her arms wide. A flock of gemeyes rose from the surrounding rocks, their plumage flashing and glinting with rainbows beneath the desert sun.

Luman gave Ali a final kiss on the cheek and stepped aside.

Tears blurred his vision. He knew that whatever happened, this was the last time he would see the old woman who had cared for and nurtured him.

The birds flocked around him.

Ali's skin tingled, the air around him thrumming, alive. Suddenly he felt light and buoyant. He spread his arms in wonder, laughing aloud as he rose into the air surrounded by a cloud of luck birds. He flew higher and higher until Luman was but a dot on the landscape. Then, with Ali held in some sort of invisible net or cocoon by the power of the gemeyes, they turned towards Afyonkarahisar.

The Bādiyah Ash-Shām rushed beneath him, hot wind ruffling his hair. He passed over glittering pans of salt, great beds of bare stone and monolithic rocky crags, vast windswept desert sands, and over forests, farmland, towns and cities, before the birds delivered him to his destination.

They set him down on the outskirts of Afyonkarahisar when the sun was low in the sky. The gemeyes fluttered around him, chirping softly. Messages of hope flashed into his mind, feelings of gratitude and love. Then they bade him farewell and before he knew it, they were mere specks in the sky, quickly disappearing from sight.

It was up to him now. Alone, he had to try to stop Savich.

He gazed in trepidation at the Black Citadel, stark and menacing atop Afyonkarahisar Hill, its Stygian ramparts and parapets silhouetted against the setting sun. The hill itself was a craggy mound of dark volcanic rock devoid of vegetation, rising more than 200 metres from the surrounding plains.

Ali took a deep breath and set off along the road towards it.

Before long he overtook three farm lads lugging heavy sacks of potatoes to the citadel. One of them, burdened with two sacks instead of just one like his companions, was lagging behind.

"They look heavy," Ali said, coming up alongside him. "Let me give you a hand."

The lad needed no convincing, and Ali was soon striding along beside him with a lumpy sack of potatoes slung across his shoulders. Even though dusk was approaching, slaves were bent working in the freshly ploughed fields either side of the road, overseers watching and cajoling them to work harder.

"They're planting poppy seeds," the lad said, seeing Ali staring at them. "Afyonkarahisar is infamous for its opium. It's how the master in the citadel funds his army."

They saw no one else on the road until they approached the fortified wall that enclosed the old town surrounding the Black Citadel. Haggard women and hungry-eyed, skinny children watched their every move from makeshift shelters that lined both sides of the road. Rotting corpses hung from the town's wall, rank and buzzing with flies.

The world seemed to spin. There was a heavy tightness in Ali's chest, and he felt the blood drain from his face. Living on the streets of Korykos, he had seen poverty and deprivation, seen brutality and bloodshed, but nothing like this. It made him feel nauseated, but he pressed on.

When they reached the town gate, an armed Uzbeg stepped from a guard box. "Halt," he ordered. "What have you got there?"

"Potatoes," said one of the farm lads.

The guard ambled around the four lads, inspecting their every detail. He stopped beside Ali, looking him up and down. Ali met his probing gaze with an assumed nonchalance, but his heart was thumping and his bowels felt weak.

"What's your name?" the guard demanded.

"Isa," Ali said, giving the first farmer's name that popped into his head.

The man continued to stare at him.

Then another guard appeared from the shadows of the gateway and stood with his legs spread and his hands on his hips. "Come on you lot, hurry along. We shut the gate at sundown."

Ali could not believe his luck. They hurried past the Uzbeg guards and through the gate. But as he walked along the road into the town, the fine hairs on the back of his neck prickled with the feeling someone was watching him.

He glanced quickly back. One of the guards was following them. Ali's legs suddenly felt like jelly, but he managed to keep walking. He did his best to act like one of the farm lads and went with them to the market area where hucksters offered grain, vegetables and other produce for sale.

He had been foolish to think he could simply walk into Afyonkarahisar. If he had any hope of stopping Savich, he had to find a way to slip away from his pursuer.

One after the other, the lads dumped their sacks of potatoes under the hessian awning of the potato stall. When it was Ali's turn, he took the opportunity to sneak another glance backwards. The gatehouse guard was now watching him from behind a stall on the other side of the street.

When the unloading was done, Ali bided his time, joking and making small talk with the farm lads. His chance came when a handcart laden high with bales of straw momentarily blocked the guard's view. Ali quickly slipped behind the potato stall awning and scuttled away on all fours behind the other stalls. When he reached the opposite end of the market, he stepped back onto the road and joined a group of shoppers heading home with their produce. He walked with his head bowed and heart thumping, half expecting a hand on his shoulder at any moment. But soon they were clear of the market with no sign of pursuit.

One by one, the market-goers turned off into buildings or lanes until Ali was the only person left still treading the paved road that climbed steadily uphill towards the Black Citadel. It made him feel conspicuous.

Voices came from further back along the road. He peered anxiously around, but could not yet see the approaching people. This section of the road was walled either side by high stone buildings, with no sign of a lane or gate. A short way ahead, however, a pile of barrels was stacked by the side of the road. He hurried over to them, found a gap and wriggled into it. There was a small space in the centre of the stack of barrels where he was able to crouch and watch the road through a narrow gap.

None too soon, because almost straight away he spied a kitchen maid and a delivery boy coming along the road, carrying a basket between them laden with dirt-caked potatoes, possibly the very ones he had carried into town. They passed by without so much as a glance in his direction, but before he could breathe a sigh of relief there was a soft thud above him.

From the top of the barrels a crow was staring down one side of its beak at him. When its malign yellow eyes met his, the crow craned forward and screeched, hopping from one foot to the other.

"*Shoo,*" he hissed in alarm.

He squirmed out from behind the barrels and jumped to his feet.

The crow screeched again and this time there was an answering cry from above.

Followed by another, and another…

A dread chill ran through him. The rooftops were swarming with carrion crows.

Suddenly the air was filled with a crescendo of screeches.

He turned one way then the other, but it was already too late.

Uzbeg guards were running towards him from the direction of the steps leading to the Black Citadel. From behind came the leering gatehouse guard, followed by another half dozen armed Uzbeg thugs.

He was trapped.

26. Bow Down Before Savich

Ali was frog-marched up the two hundred or more steep stone steps that led to the citadel. He passed through three levels of heavily guarded ramparts protecting the keep before they reached the top, and realised the hopelessness of his quest. It would have been impossible for him to reach the castle without being captured.

At the top, the guards dragged him none too gently across the stone-flagged courtyard and through an imposing ceremonial entrance. Inside the Black Citadel they propelled him along dark corridors and through a huge double doorway into a magnificent chamber.

Ali gazed around the room.

It was a vast, windowless assembly room, illuminated by crystal columns filled with floating sluglows. On either side of the chamber grand black-marble staircases swept up to the second floor. The walls were draped with lavish tapestries and carpets, and the floor was tiled with polished onyx flagstones.

In the centre and towards the rear of the chamber there was a black stone dais upon which stood a carven throne inlaid with gold and precious stones. Behind the throne, voluminous deep-purple drapes hung from ceiling to floor.

A sable-caped figure was seated upon the throne.

Ali was half marched, half shoved across the room: the guards' boots ringing on the polished stone, his own bare feet making hardly a whisper. Behind them, the heavy doors were slammed shut and bolted with a metallic *clunk*.

"Bow in the presence of the Master," one of his Uzbeg captors bellowed and cast him to the floor.

Ali slumped there, looking down at the polished black tiles, his jaw clenched, his stomach tight. Laughter rang out in the chamber. A mocking theatrical laugh tinged with a cold, hard edge.

Ali lifted his head and fear and loathing welled up within him. He held his breath, imagined charging at Savich, grabbing his throat and choking him.

The hideous laughter stopped and two black pits peered back at Ali from a hairless, puffy round head. The eyes, if there were any, were set so deeply in the pallid face they were lost to scrutiny.

"Welcome, Ali," Savich said in a cold, dry voice.

Ali's eyes went wide.

"Yes, I recognise you, young man. Your reputation precedes you." Savich took a sip from a small ceramic cup, motioning the guards away with his free hand. "Get up, boy, I don't want you grovelling. I want you as an ally. Come, stand before me. Have some spiced tea, perhaps?"

One of the guards lifted him to his feet.

Ali rejected Savich's words with a curt shake of his head. The gemeye memories about this man's atrocities welled up within him. He felt sick in his stomach.

The guard shoved him towards the bloated figure.

"I have had you brought here," Savich said, "to offer you your heart's desires."

Ali glared at him.

"You don't believe me? I can make you a prince, offer you wealth and power beyond your wildest dreams. Imagine that, Ali. From beggar to noble. We can help each other, you and I."

Savich clapped his hands twice and a male servant dressed in a grey, knee-length surcoat appeared from the folds of the purple curtains.

"Make our guest comfortable and bring refreshments," Savich ordered.

The servant left, only to reappear almost immediately carrying a plump, gaudily embroidered cushion under each arm. Behind him followed a servant woman bearing a small, low wooden table of fruit, sweetmeats and a steaming cup of spiced mint tea. The man placed the cushions beside Ali, the woman put the table of food and drink in front of him, and they both departed.

"Sit, lad," Savich said. "Have some tea, some sweetmeats."

Ali sat, but ignored the food.

"What I propose," Savich continued in his dry, lifeless voice, "is a new empire. A single mighty realm forged by a firm, decisive hand…my hand."

"You have no right," Ali said.

Savich leaned forward and peered hard into Ali's face. "On the contrary, it is my birthright. I am Mehmed's *older* brother. He calls himself Sultan, but he cheated the empire from me. I should have been Sultan. I *will* be Sultan, and with your dreams to aid me I will be *invincible*. I will be emperor of the world!"

He sounded insane, drunk on power.

Ali glared at him.

"Together, we can defeat all my brothers. They are pretenders. Mehmed, Suleyman, Musa, Isa, Mustafa… They are nothing but ants under my feet. Nothing, I tell you."

Savich lounged back on the magnificent throne, and chuckled knowingly at some secret thought. "I will remember and reward those allies who help me to achieve my rightful due. Join me, boy, and I will treat you like a…like a son. You can allow your imagination to run wild, choose your own reward. Join me… *Prince* Ali."

Ali sensed some force beyond his comprehension at work. Savich revolted and frightened him, and yet he found himself considering the proposal. He momentarily forgot this evil man had murdered his mother, forgot about Rose, his father, Luman and Demetri, picturing himself instead triumphant at Savich's side, even though he knew in his heart that the man was worse than a tyrant.

"Drink the tea, boy," Savich urged. "It will refresh you."

Ali reached for the cup the servant had brought him, despite having already decided not to eat or drink anything. His hand moved of its own accord. He stared at it with a dazed look, a sudden chill running though him. Even when he tried to resist, to pull his hand back, it continued to reach for the tea.

"That's the way," Savich said. "Drink. A toast." He was leaning forward eagerly, his hands on the massive arms of his throne, triumph creeping into his expression. "Go on," he urged, "drink to your new riches, to our special alliance."

Ali stared into the black pits where the man's eyes should have been, held in thrall. He tried to resist Savich's will, but his hand grasped the cup and manoeuvred it towards his mouth.

His lips parted…

Then a splinter of icy pain exploded in Ali's head.

A gemeye message.

A single brief vision that flashed so quickly through his mind he did not have time to *see* it. Instead he felt its message in his heart and soul.

It said: *Resist*.

And he did. With all his might. Sweat broke out on his brow and his arm trembled. At first nothing happened. Then, at the last moment, he halted the cup just short of his mouth.

"Drink it, boy," Savich commanded.

He had resisted Savich as the faceless man in his dreams, so he could do it again.

Summoning all his strength, all his will, his hand trembling, he managed to lower the cup a little. He shot a glance from left to right to make sure the guards had retreated. Then he screeched at the top of his lungs, a piercing cry that startled Savich and guards alike.

It was no cry of anguish, but a more than passable imitation of a swamp owl. Good enough to fool the floating sluglows who blinked out and thudded to the bottom of their crystal columns.

The windowless room was plunged into total darkness.

Ali threw the cup of tea aside, and it smashed loudly on the stone floor. Then he padded softly in the opposite direction. He made his way towards the right-hand staircase, its image still vivid in his mind's eye. The noise of the guards' bellowing and blundering covered any small sound he might have made as his hand came in contact with the banister, and he moved swiftly up the stairs.

He paused on the landing at the top of the stairs, his heart pounding, and noticed a faint glow, barely discernible, coming from a narrow side passage ahead of him.

Down below, Savich was chanting an incantation.

Suddenly there was a loud *pop* and an eerie red light shone from the lower chamber.

Ali flung himself into the side passage and fled along it until he came to a corridor illuminated by a feeble oil lamp set in a niche in the wall.

Behind him the clomp of booted footsteps sounded on the stairs.

He turned frantically from left to right, his heart racing even harder, only to find both ends of the corridor blocked by stout doors.

He hurried to the door at his left and tried the handle but it was locked.

He dashed to the other door and desperately shook the handle… but it, too, was locked. For a dreadful moment despair threatened to overwhelm him, then he realised with a gush of relief that the key was protruding from the lock.

In the narrow passage behind him, heavy footfalls and gruff voices rapidly approached.

He eased the lock open as quietly as he could, removed the key, and slipped backwards through the door, bending to close and lock it behind him.

But as he straightened, he sensed movement and barely managed to duck aside as a heavy brass candelabra swished down and struck him a glancing blow on the shoulder.

He whirled to face his assailant, their eyes met and he froze.

In that same moment, his attacker—an unnaturally pale teenage girl with dark smudges beneath fearful almond-shaped green eyes—also froze, arm drawn back to strike again.

"Rose!" Ali cried in astonishment.

27. A Rose by Any Other Name

The girl lowered her weapon hesitantly, her eyes growing wide. She blinked and stared incredulously at him. "Ali?"

He rubbed his shoulder gingerly. "Must you attack me every time we meet?"

"And I suppose you've come to rescue me again?" she countered. "Because that worked out so well the other times."

"Yes, no… I mean… Actually, I didn't know you were in here. I was trying to escape from Savich. But now that I've found you, we can escape together."

Her bottom lip trembled. She let the candelabra drop to the floor and threw her arms around his neck, her face pressed into his shoulder.

Her body felt warm and soft against his. He ran his fingers through her hair.

"Oh, Ali," she said, leaning back and peering into his face. "I don't think you or anyone can save me."

Then someone rattled the door from outside, trying to open it.

"Lady Ashye," came Savich's wheedling voice. "Let me in."

Ali shot Rose a questioning glance.

"Lady Ashye, open the door. I know Ali is in there with you." There was a pause, then Savich spoke more sternly. "I want him. Unlock the door now or I will open it my way."

"*You?*" Ali said. "You're the Lady Ashye?" His mind reeled. "But you told me your name was Rose."

She dropped her gaze. "Sorry, I lied. I was trying to hide my real identity."

Ali shook his head at her duplicity. "I suspected, but your father dismissed my suggestion." It all made sense now, that this slave girl—his Rose—was actually *the* Lady Ashye. "But I thought you and I…" Realising the hopelessness of his feelings for her, his voice trailed off.

She looked at him. "Thought what?"

He shook his head in denial. "Nothing, it's silly, *Lady* Ashye…"

"Call me Rose, I prefer it, it's my favourite flower. Now tell me."

"I thought, you know… I thought that you and I…"

"What?" she urged.

He pulled her close to him again. "I told you last time, Rose. I can't stop thinking about you."

"Me too," she admitted, falling into his embrace. "I can't stop thinking about you either. I thought I would never see you again, never be able to tell you how I feel."

Her cheek was smooth and soft against his own. Her body trembled in his arms. He took gentle hold of her face and kissed her, her soft lips melting beneath his own.

Then he broke away, breathing a little heavier than usual.

She gazed at him, her lips moist and half parted.

"I want to wed you," he murmured.

Her green eyes glistened with unshed tears. "It can never be, Ali."

He gave her a pained stare. "Why?"

"Because my father won't allow it. I am…I am to be wed to a great man, a man of royal blood."

His face reddened. "You are betrothed?"

"No. Yes. Kind of," she said in a rush.

He stepped back from her, raising his palms in a questioning shrug. "What does that mean?"

She let out a heavy sigh. "My birth was apparently an auspicious event. They say that a pair of luck birds came to watch over my mother when she was in labour and when I was born they sang a gemeye birdsong duet."

Ali frowned, trying to recall if he had seen this event in the gemeyes' collective memory.

"The birdsong was a portent. It foretold that I will one day wed a leader of men. A man of royal blood, of power and wisdom. Everyone who heard the song heard the message in their minds. That's why I ran away and changed my name to Rose."

"Because of a bird's song?"

"You don't understand. I have had to live with this hanging over me my whole life. Everyone knows and expects me to fulfil the promise."

"But I love you, Rose." His voice was strained.

She shook her head. "It can never be." She bit her lip and turned away. "I'm sorry, Ali. You're just an orphan from the streets."

"Which is why," Savich's voice suddenly interrupted from the other side of the bolted door, "you and I are the perfect match, Lady Ashye."

The star-crossed young couple looked hopelessly around the room. For a moment they had blotted out the threat of Savich, caught up in their reunion and what it revealed. But now the dire predicament of their situation urgently reasserted itself. The only way in or out of the room was via the locked door, a red light glowing around its edges and piercing through the keyhole.

Ali recognised it as the same unnatural light he had seen in the lower chamber after the sluglows had gone out. It became brighter and brighter until it was so intense that it burned like molten metal.

"Stand back," Ali cried. He snatched the heavy brass candleholder from where Rose had dropped it. He weighed it in his hand and turned to face the door.

Suddenly the door bulged unnaturally, cracking and splintering. Then it exploded in a mighty crash, as though some massive iron-shod battering ram had been employed on it. Chunks of wood shot into the room. A piece the size of a man's fist struck Ali in the face, making his nose bleed, and both he and Rose were peppered with stinging splinters.

Red light flooded into the room and Savich stepped into the open doorway, bloated and laughing. "A clever trick, boy, but it will do you no good." There was venom in his voice.

Ali held the candleholder like a cudgel, blood running over

his lips and down his chin.

"Drop it!" Savich commanded.

Ali had meant to strike him, but instead, against his will, his hand released the candelabra and it clattered to the floor.

Savich gave a low, icy chuckle. "Bring them both to the throne room," he ordered, and turned away with a swirl of his midnight-black sable cape.

The guards treated Rose with some modicum of respect, but Ali they treated with contempt, half shoving and half knocking him along the narrow passage and down the stairs. On the lower level, now lit by flaming torches held aloft by servants and fitted into sconces on the walls, he was dragged across the chamber and cast onto the floor alongside another prisoner sprawled on the cold, black floor.

Rose was led onto the dais and forced to kneel at Savich's feet. She cowered there, gazing at Ali in barely suppressed terror.

Ali looked away, unable to hold her in his gaze. He felt responsible for their predicament, impotent and ashamed. His eyes fell on the battered and bruised form of the figure beside him.

The stranger rolled over and groaned, the shackles chaining his ankles rattling with the movement. His face was swollen and bloody, his lips split, his one eye half closed and blackened…

His *one* eye…

The fine hairs stood up on the back of Ali's neck. He stared at the battered face, his mind reducing the swelling, wiping the blood away, discolouring the bruises…

"Demetri!" he cried, but a swift kick from one of the guards silenced him.

The battered boy tried to speak, but the effort made him wince.

Savich sneered. "A touching reunion, Ali. Do not fear, we shall attend to your young friend shortly. But first I want you to have the pleasure of watching while I attend to Erkan, your *father*, once and for all."

Ali glared at him, gritting his teeth in an effort to calm himself so he could think clearly.

Savich clapped three times and the curtains behind him parted.

Fedar entered the chamber bearing a wire cage in one hand and a silver chalice in the other. Imprisoned in the cage was a dull-eyed, cringing gemeye.

Ali gasped, struck by the awful realisation of what Savich was about to do. He lurched to his feet, but he was felled by a savage blow from the guard behind him.

"*Cehenneme git!*" Ali swore at Fedar. *Go to hell*!

Fedar shuffled forward, glancing at Ali with hooded eyes, and proffered the chalice to Savich.

Savich accepted it and with his free hand he drew a black-handled dagger from the scabbard at his waist. He raised both the dagger and chalice high in the air like a shaman performing a magic ritual.

Fedar went to the wire cage and withdrew the gemeye, its crystalline plumage dull and lustreless, drained of colour, and proffered it to his master. Savich held the chalice beneath the bird and raised the blade above it.

Rose gave a weak cry and Savich responded with a sinister chuckle.

Ali gagged and swallowed back the vomit rising in his throat.

"This," Savich hissed, "is the end for Erkan and Mehmed. Luman is dead and in two days, Lady Ashye, you will be my wife and I shall be on the Beyler Palace throne in Amasya." He gave a leer.

Shock and outrage sent Ali's mind reeling.

Luman dead… It could not be.

The end for his father and the Sultan.

Rose married to Savich.

Savich made Sultan.

Then the gemeye in Fedar's bony grasp used the last of its strength to touch Ali's mind.

In that instant, Ali knew it was true. Knew Luman was dead. But gone though she was, Ali heard her words echo in his mind, remembered and relayed by the weakened gemeye. She told him that he was the only one who could defeat Savich.

Ali licked his lips and glanced at Rose.

She made a pleading, whimpering sound.

At that, Savich laughed in triumph and brought the blade of the dagger down towards the throat of the helpless gemeye.

28. The Sapphire Mist

"Stop!" Ali shrieked.

It came from deep within him, from the fundamental core of his very soul. It racked him in a violent shudder and set off something that coursed through him like an electric shock, a pulse that momentarily both paralysed and blinded him.

When it passed and his vision cleared, he found himself looking at the room through a sapphire mist and realised that something very strange had happened. A quick glance around the chamber revealed that everybody in the room except for him was paralysed, completely frozen in the moment of his scream.

For a second or two he was confused, then it dawned on him: he had passed into a waking dream state. He had stepped out of time and was dream weaving.

His mouth was filled with the taste of copper.

When he realised what was happening, Ali strode over to Savich and wrenched the dagger from the evil man's petrified grip. His intention had been to disarm him, but with the dagger in his hand and fury raging in his heart, a dark thought crept into his mind. He weighed the weapon in his hand, feeling its balance, noting the keenness of its edge, the sharpness of its point.

He looked into Savich's pasty face and stared into the black pits of his eyes, gemeye memories of the man's evil deeds fuelling his outrage and disgust. Ali gently pressed the point of the dagger to Savich's throat. It would be so easy to plunge the wicked blade into the artery that was still pulsing in the otherwise inert man's neck.

This man had killed Luman. Had killed his mother. Was killing his father. And planned to force Rose to marry him and use the gemeye prophecy to help legitimise his claim to the throne.

Rose…

It would be so simple, Ali thought, the dagger comfortable in his hand.

He grieved for Luman, and in doing so he wondered what the old woman would have done in his place. As a Dream Weaver, what did she expect him to do?

Ali looked at the dagger.

It would be so simple…

His knuckles had turned white around its hilt. A tiny trickle of blood ran from the tip of the blade where it had pricked the skin of Savich's pale neck.

At the sight of the blood, Ali snatched back the dagger and dropped it clattering to the stone floor.

He could not do it. Could not bring himself to kill the man, no matter how evil he was.

Revenge was not the answer. Murder was not the answer.

Two wrongs *do not* make a right.

In the end, it was the images of Savich's own bloodthirsty murders and ritual slaying of the gemeyes, still sickeningly fresh in Ali's mind, that ultimately helped him reject the temptation.

Instead, Ali turned to free the helpless luck bird still caught in Fedar's grip. He prised open the old man's stiff, bony fingers and the bedraggled bird fluttered into the air—somehow free of the constraints of his dream—and he was filled by the warm glow of the bird's gratitude.

Ali gazed into Fedar's frozen face. Not so long ago he had wanted to kill him too, but now all the contempt and hatred had drained away. He was still angry with him; how could he not be? But he also felt a little sorry for the misguided old man. He knew Fedar was a scoundrel and a betrayer, but he also remembered times of kindness shown by the old man when Ali was young. He remembered games, learning mathematics on his knee, times when Fedar protected and stood up for him.

But what was real, and what was an act, and how much of

what Fedar did was because Savich ordered him? To think he'd once looked up to Fedar and admired the man. It made him sick to even remember those feelings.

He went next to Rose and knelt at her side, but a rasping sound from behind brought him up short. He got back to his feet and turned to face Savich's still frozen form.

Or *was* he still frozen?

Ali stepped close to the man he had once thought of as his nemesis and searched his puffy features. Way down deep, within Savich's sunken eyes, unnatural pinpricks of red light glowed like tiny burning coals.

Ali backed away warily, a sudden cold dread knotting the pit of his stomach.

Even as he watched, the corner of Savich's mouth twitched, and Ali knew he was trying to break free of the dream.

Without consciously calling it up, a picture of Rose's father came alive in Ali's mind. Like the time when he had first seen him in İskenderūn, Omar Agha was at the head of a Janissary cavalry troop. Except this time, he was not in İskenderūn but right here on the outskirts of Afyonkarahisar. The search for his daughter had brought him here in the nick of time, and Ali reached out to him in his dream, calling him to the Black Citadel.

In his dream imagination Ali saw a gemeye alight on the Agha's shoulder, and incredibly, at the very same moment, the bird Ali had freed from Fedar's frozen clutches landed on his own.

In that moment Ali knew his call for help had been received, and the dream vision faded.

He cast a glance at Savich, whose sunken eyes now burned with malignant power. Ali felt beads of sweat break out on his forehead. His heart was in his throat. He had to save Rose. He had a vague notion of physically carrying her away, but before he could act, the rasping sound he had heard moments ago came again, and he realised Savich was trying to speak.

Savich's deep eyes came alive, blazing like red-hot coals, and his mouth twisted into a sneer. He raised his hand in slow jerks, breaking free of the paralysis, pointing a clawed finger at him.

Ali gasped.

"You will pay for this," Savich croaked. "I will—"

"*No*!" Ali screamed.

Savich froze again before he could finish what he was about to say. But the sinister red light remained in his eyes, burning brighter and brighter, until his eyes became white hot and began to consume his face.

The fiery light spread, bubbling and popping like molten lava, sizzling tendrils coursing through Savich's body and along his limbs. It crackled and fizzed with the stench of brimstone, consuming him bit by bit. Finally, there was a loud *whoosh*, like the sound of Greek fire igniting, and Savich burst into flame, flooding the room with dazzling red light.

Ali was forced to cover his eyes and look away. The gemeye on his shoulder flitted away, hovering some distance high above them. By the time the searing brightness had faded enough for Ali too look back, it was over.

What remained of Savich still stood momentarily frozen in the same pointing attitude—a dull, blackened parody of the former man—then the figure crumbled, falling away until it collapsed into a pile of ash.

At the same time, Ali's own misty sapphire haze began to fade. He glanced around the room. One of the guards blinked his eyes, Demetri groaned, and Fedar twitched a couple of times.

The vibrancy was gone from the air.

The dream was over.

29. The Fallout

Gruff voices and the heavy tread of booted feet sounded in the corridors of the Black Citadel. Demetri and Rose looked at Ali, neither sure what was happening. Savich's Uzbeg guards were gaping at the ashen remains of their ex-master.

Fedar, however, wasted no time worrying about Savich. The moment Ali's dream was over and time had returned to normal, Fedar took stock of the situation and scurried across the floor to snatch up Savich's fallen dagger.

Beyond the chamber, men were approaching the door.

Fedar licked his lips, his gaze flicking from Ali to the stairs to the door and back to Ali.

"Where's my father," Ali demanded.

The door to the chamber crashed open and Omar Agha strode into the room, curved-blade sword drawn. Armed Janissaries streamed in behind him, quickly restraining the dazed Uzbeg guards.

Almost oblivious to these events, the Agha had halted mid-step, momentarily transfixed by the sight of his missing daughter. Then he broke free of the thrall, sheathed his sword and swept her into his arms. He hugged Rose to his broad chest, whispering gentle words to soothe her shuddering sobs.

Still brandishing the dagger, Fedar was edging towards the staircase.

Ali took a step towards him. "Where is my father?"

"Don't come any closer," Fedar said, threatening him with the blade.

"Drop your weapon or I will shoot," shouted a Janissary who

had brought his bow and arrow to bear.

Sweat broke out on Fedar's forehead.

"Give me the dagger," Ali said, stepping forward with his hand outstretched. He was not afraid of his one-time friend and former mentor, not anymore, but now he was afraid *for* him.

Fedar licked his lips again, then turned to flee up the stairs.

"No," Ali cried.

In the same instant there was a soft *swish,* followed by a meaty *thud,* and Fedar dropped before he had even managed two steps, an arrow impaling his chest.

Ali rushed to where Fedar lay slumped on the stairs and knelt at his side.

Fedar let out a long sigh. His mouth worked but no sound came forth, only a blood-pink bubble which popped on his lips.

Their eyes met.

"Forgive me," Fedar managed in a voice so faint it was barely a whisper.

Ali took his hand. "If you ever cared anything for me, Fedar, please tell me where my father is."

Fedar's mouth worked, but all that emerged was a gurgle. Then the skull-faced old man wilted and his head lolled.

Ali got to his feet, hung his own head and said a few words of prayer. A pair of Janissary infantrymen stepped around him, hefted Fedar's lifeless form and carried him away.

Demetri limped over to Ali to comfort him.

"If we don't find my father soon," Ali said, "I'm afraid we'll be too late. We may already be too late."

It was then that the bedraggled gemeye Ali had released from Fedar's clutches fluttered down from on high where it had observed events and came to perch on Demetri's shoulder.

"Bird," Demetri said in greeting. Noticing a change in Ali's features, he asked, "What's wrong?"

But Ali was studying the gemeye. Its eyes were dull and its feathers were the colour of weathered lead. The bird made eye contact and a wave of fatigue washed over him.

He sniffed and wiped his nose with the back of his hand. "This has been an ordeal for your luck bird, Demetri."

The gemeye leaned over and pressed its head against Demetri's cheek, then gave a feeble squawk and fluttered back into the air and out through the now open door.

"Bird!" Demetri cried.

Ali clutched his friend's arm. "It's all right, Bird will come back to you. But for the moment he is ailing and needs to seek succour with his own kind."

Demetri gave him a quizzical look. "When did you become an expert on luck birds?"

Ali smiled. "Trust me. Bird will come back to you."

The two lads now stood together, trying not to eavesdrop on the intimate words of love and regret that passed between the reunited father and daughter. Finally, the Agha turned from his daughter and strode across the room to the small heap of ash and kicked some aside with his toe.

"This is truly Savich?" the Agha asked, narrowing his eyes.

Rose glanced at Ali. "Yes, father. What's left of him."

The Agha turned to Ali. "We meet again, young man. My daughter tells me you did this."

Ali gave him a weak smile.

The Agha narrowed his eyes. "How?"

"I think Savich's blood magic backfired on him. Thank Luman."

"Yes, thank Luman indeed." The Agha scrutinised Ali before embracing him in a formal manner, then released him and stepped away. "If you indeed had a hand in this, young man, the realm owes you a great debt. *I* owe you a great debt."

Ali shrugged and stared down at his hands.

Omar Agha looked hard at him. "What's wrong, lad? Is it your friend? The girl you were looking for. Is she here? Is she safe?"

Ali nodded glumly.

The Agha clapped him on the back. "Then cheer up. Name your reward and I will do everything in my power to grant it."

Rose tugged at her father's sleeve and whispered into his ear.

The Agha's face went slack, the colour draining from it. He pulled off his tall felt cap and ran his fingers through his thick black hair, a sudden weariness in his eyes. He turned to face Ali again.

"Is the girl you were looking for my daughter?" he demanded.

Ali swallowed. "Yes, Rose—I mean, the Lady Ashye—is the girl I love."

The Agha's face went red. "That's impossible."

"I know," Ali said. "Which is why I am walking away. It would be too dangerous for her to be with me. But before I go I ask that you please help me find my father. I believe he is imprisoned here."

The Agha was visibly relieved that Ali was not pressing for his daughter's hand, but was also puzzled and perhaps a little suspicious. After a moment, he said, "All right, I will instruct my men to stay and help you search."

Rose turned to Ali, her face flushed, her green eyes ablaze. "What do you mean? Are you saying you don't want me?"

Ali sighed. "Of course I want you. It's just…"

She put her hands on her hips. "Just what? Another girl?"

"There's no other girl," Ali said, rolling his eyes.

"Then come with me."

Ali shook his head. "I can't. You don't know what I am. I'm dangerous."

"I don't understand," she said, her lip trembling. "I thought you wanted to be with me."

"Ashye," the Agha said. "The gemeye prophecy. This boy is not for you. You are to marry a great man, a man of royal blood."

"My mistake," she retorted. "I thought Ali was a great man." She thrust her chin forward. "As you wish, father. I will wed whoever you choose."

"But you said you wouldn't do that," Ali said. "You told me that was why you ran away."

"Seems that I lied," she replied coldly.

"Not for the first time it seems, *Lady* Ashye," he retorted.

"Come, father!" She stomped from the room, leaving Ali standing there dumbfounded, staring at the empty doorway.

"Are you going to go after her?" Demetri asked.

At first Ali did not answer, then he pulled himself together. "No, I have to find my father. He's got to be here somewhere."

"What about Rose?"

"What about her?" Ali said, folding his arms across his chest, his eyes cold.

30. Death and Rebirth

The captain of the Janissaries stood facing Ali under the portico at the entrance to the Black Citadel. It was still half dark outside, morning twilight, the sun not yet visible on the horizon.

"Your father is not here," the captain said. "My men have spent hours turning this place upside down and inside out. You saw them, you helped."

"He *is* here," Ali said. "I can feel his presence. But we have to hurry because he is fading."

"I'm sorry, there's nothing more we can do." The captain turned away and descended the portico steps to the courtyard. "I have other duties to attend to, the empire is still in dire peril."

Ali followed him.

Demetri remained under the portico, leaning on a walking stick.

"Omar Agha told you to stay and help me find him," Ali said, his arms hanging at his sides.

The captain gave Ali a regretful look. "I'm truly sorry, but we've done all we can."

Without another word, the captain turned, headed across the courtyard and down the stone steps leading from the Black Citadel, his men falling in behind and following him two by two.

Ali watched them depart, then sniffed and climbed back up the steps. "I can feel him, Demetri. My father is here and he is still alive, but only just."

"You said you saw him in a dream. Try to remember the details."

"Don't you think I have?" Ali snapped. "I've racked my memory for anything that might help me find him."

"Give it another shot," Demetri said. "Try describing it to me. Where was he when you saw him?"

Ali rubbed a hand over his face. "I told you. On a rack in a dungeon."

Demetri nodded encouragement. "Could you hear anything?"

Ali shook his head.

"Could you smell anything?"

Besides fear and pain? he thought. He shrugged. "Maybe a whiff of something, like hot metal."

"Was it light or dark?"

Ali blinked, then his eyes went wide. "That's *it,* Demetri! There was an unnatural red light. Savich's sorcery. The entrance is hidden by Savich's blood magic."

They hurried back into the Black Citadel and Ali moved from room to room, using some sixth sense, an ability that had developed when he and his father connected via their dreams. Finally, he came to a halt near the left-hand wall of the throne chamber where Savich had burned to ash.

"This is where I feel his presence the strongest," he said.

But there was nothing to be seen. The Janissaries had ripped the tapestries and carpets from the walls revealing only solid masonry, and the polished black tiles on the floor had proved to be immovable.

Ali closed his eyes and stood there, breathing slowly, centring himself. He reached out to Tengri, not with his mind but with his heart, with his very being. The emotions bottled inside him poured out: anger and grief at Luman's murder, fear for his father, heartache for Rose, frustration and guilt at his own inability to act…

It was a cry for help.

Suddenly a blinding pulse, a spasm of energy, coursed through him. When his vision returned, he found himself looking at the wall through a radiant sapphire mist, his mouth filled with the taste of copper.

A blue dreamlight revealed a stout wooden door set in the stonework of the wall. A door that had previously been invisible.

He gave it a push and it swung open to reveal steps descending into a dark cellar. The air was damp and rank.

Ali hurried down the slimy, moss-covered steps and paused at the bottom to get his bearings. It was the same cellar as the one in the dream he had shared with his ailing father. He crossed swiftly to the back corner of the cellar and wrenched open the wooden trapdoor in the floor.

A rank odour wafted up.

Ali lowered himself into the cell.

The blue-tinged dreamlight illuminated the room.

His father hung naked and emaciated—shackled by his wrists and ankles, his toes and fingers dark with dried blood—on Savich's torture rack. His head was held up by an iron band across his forehead, but there was no sign of life.

Ali stifled a sob.

Demetri stepped up beside him. "Is he alive?"

Ali moved to his father's side and felt for a heartbeat. "Barely. Quick, we have to get him out before the dream ends and the door disappears again."

Ali removed the iron band around his father's head while Demetri released the levers fastening the iron shackles that pinned Erkan to the rack.

Free of restraints, Erkan's body slumped forward into their waiting arms and they hefted his unconscious form up the two flights of steps and into the throne chamber.

Even as they stumbled into the room, Ali felt the dream leave him. A wave of fatigue washed over him and the sapphire mist evaporated.

They lowered Ali's father's unconscious form gently onto the polished black floor tiles and sagged down beside him, breathing heavily. Ali brushed the hair from his father's forehead and peered into his face.

Erkan was deathly thin and pale.

Ali began to weep softly.

This man was his father. Even though they had not seen each other since he was a baby—save his encounters with the peculiar sailor and the Wandering Pilgrim—he *knew* him and loved him.

His union with the gemeyes, with Tengri, had allowed him to know his father more intimately than if they had never been separated.

"Let's get him out into the sunlight," Ali said. "It must be dawn by now."

They took hold of him, one under each arm, and lugged him across the chamber, his heels dragging along the floor, out onto the front porch beneath the portico of the Black Citadel, and down the stairs to the courtyard. The sun was low and red in the sky, the clouds bronzed.

The daylight lifted Ali's spirits.

But when they laid his father on the flagstones, Ali froze in terror. The surrounding rooftops were swarming with birds. *Carrion crows!* he thought. Then he laughed in relief because he realised that the birds were gemeyes.

Ali saw them and they saw him and their minds became as one.

"Rejoice," their trilling voices sounded in his head, "rejoice."

The gemeyes rose into the air and descended into the courtyard, blanketing Erkan, their emerald eyes sparkling and flashing.

"Luman is dead. Long live Luman," they continued. Feelings of love, loss, compassion and healing overwhelmed him. The gemeyes grieved for the loss of the old woman who called herself Sister, but accepted her departure knowing that she was now one with the warm light of Tengri.

Then the gemeyes raised his father into the air and happiness and relief flooded through him.

"Long live Luman," went their song.

Ali understood.

Not only was his father going to survive, but Tengri had chosen him to become the new Luman, the protector of the people.

The birds hovered in a cloud above the courtyard, Erkan held aloft in their midst, and showered Ali with gratitude and love.

"Farewell, Dream Weaver," came their parting message. "Dream well."

Then the gemeyes turned as one with Erkan, now Luman, cradled amongst them and flew south-east towards Bādiyah Ash-

Shām, the immense arid desert.

But when they had gone one gemeye remained.

Demetri's "Bird" had returned, full of sparkle and colour once more, and it alighted on the one-eyed boy's shoulder.

31. One Month Later

"It's locked," Demetri said, rattling the stout iron-shod gate. "What do we do now? The wall is too high, impossible to climb."

They were standing in the outer gardens of the Beyler Palace in the city of Amasya, on the northern bank of the Yeşilırmak River, high in the mountains above the Black Sea. It was a clear, sunny day and the garden air was scented with the perfume of roses and sweet basil.

Ali scratched his head. The gate was the only entrance in the tall stone wall that fenced the famous maze and inner buildings of the Sultan's palace. "How should I know?" he said irritably, turning to look back the way they had come.

Palace gardeners in yellow caps were busy, planting hyacinth bulbs, harvesting bright red autumn apples, and tidying garden beds.

Demetri gave him a sidelong glance and muttered something under his breath. Bird moved restlessly on his shoulder.

Ali thrust out his chest and glared at him. "What did you call me?"

"A love-lost fool," Demetri said. "You're pining for that girl, Rose."

Ali clenched his teeth.

A pair of young lovers came strolling through the celebrated gardens towards them. "Look," said the wide-eyed young woman. "That fellow has a luck bird on his shoulder."

"It's not bringing us much luck today," Demetri said. "We

can't open the gate into the maze."

The young man laughed. "The palace has a main entrance on the other side of the gardens, you know. It's a lot easier than the maze, assuming you can get past the palace guards."

The young woman elbowed him and turned to Ali and Demetri. "Legend has it that a person must be both loyal of heart and lucky by nature to enter the maze."

"How does this gate mechanism work?" Ali asked. "What's one supposed to do?"

"Press a coin into the lock and give the handle a twist," she said. "If you are deemed worthy, it will open."

"But even if you could open the gate," the young man said, "they say the maze is unfathomable. Haunted by *jinn* and the ghosts of those who thought otherwise."

The young woman tried to hit him again, but he ran off laughing and she chased after him, laughing too.

Ali peered closely at the lock. He unslung the luck coin from around his neck and examined it. One face of the coin was minted with the image of a luck bird, and his heart leaped when he recognised it as the same image engraved into the circular recess of the brass lock on the gate.

He pressed the coin into the recess and it fitted perfectly. He gave the handle a twist. At first nothing happened, then there was a metallic click, followed by the whirr of a clockwork mechanism. Ali withdrew the coin and the gate swung open. They slipped through and found themselves standing in a pebbled clearing with three separate paths leading in different directions into a tall boxwood maze.

The clockwork mechanism whirred and the gate clicked ominously shut behind them.

Demetri glanced apprehensively at him.

Ali grinned. "I know the way." He turned the luck coin over and showed Demetri the pattern on the other side. "It's a puzzle. I've done it dozens of times."

Demetri's eyes went wide. "Is it the maze?"

"I'm pretty sure," Ali said.

He used the luck coin to navigate their way along the twisting and turning interconnecting paths. Despite the young lovers' warning, there were no ghosts or *jinn*. In fact, if not for the gravity of their visit, it would have been a rather pleasant stroll. When they reached the centre of the hedge puzzle, Ali and Demetri emerged into a rectangular garden of flowering rose bushes set around a large marble pool with a bubbling fountain. The garden was divided into quarters by pebbled paths that radiated from the central plaza around the pool, and exited the garden through archways in the perimeter hedge.

"Look, there's a person over there," Demetri said.

In a garden bed over to their right, a young man was cutting roses. He was clean-shaven, of medium height and a little stout, dressed in a simple white kaftan and turban. He moved from one plant to the next, deftly avoiding the thorns, searching for the best of the long-stemmed red roses. When he found a suitable specimen, he cut it from the bush, examined the bloom and smelled its perfume, before adding it to the bunch on the lawn at his feet.

Ali hailed him and made his way to where the man was working. "Are you the gardener?" he asked.

The young man gave him a bemused smile. "Yes, that too, among other things. You could say I'm the caretaker here. There is always so much to do." He peered questioningly at the two lads. "Is there something I can help you with?"

"I'm looking for a man called Kirisci," Ali said.

"And you are…?" the young man asked, his thick black eyebrows raised.

"I'm Ali and this is Demetri."

"How did you find your way through the maze?" The young man studied the boys. "It's supposed to be impossible."

"With this," Ali said, holding up the luck coin. "It was my father's."

The young man looked at it and nodded. "I am the one you seek. Only a select few know me as Kirisci, it is my private name. Most know me as Mehmed."

Demetri gasped and dropped to one knee. "Your Imperial Majesty," he said, bowing his head.

Ali frowned at Demetri. What was his friend doing? Was it possible this amiable gardener was the Sultan? "But you're not much older than us," he said, dropping to his knee and bowing just in case.

"Please rise," Mehmed said kindly, an amused smile twisting his lips.

When they stood, Demetri's gemeye companion—Bird—made a kind of soft cooing sound. Sultan Mehmed held out his hand and the gemeye fluttered from Demetri's shoulder to land on his raised finger.

Any remaining doubt that this was the Sultan drained from Ali. He gulped and said, "I am afraid that I must advise you, Your Majesty, that I killed your brother Savich."

Sultan Mehmed nodded sagely. "Yes, you defeated my brother. My *evil* brother. But dead, who knows?"

"He turned to ashes before my very eyes," Ali said.

Mehmed stared off into the distance. "Luman showed me in my dreams what took place. Whatever happened to him in the end, he did it to himself. Though whether it was self-immolation or some form of escape, we may never know."

The gemeye launched itself from the Sultan's finger, squawking in shrill tones, its eyes flashing emerald as it swooped and dived above them like some aerial circus performer.

Then, to Ali's amazement, Sultan Mehmed went down on one knee and bowed before *him*. Demetri grabbed Mehmed's arm and tried to help him to his feet, but the Sultan shrugged him off.

"I recognise you as a Dream Weaver, Ali," Sultan Mehmed said. "And I ask that you grant me the honour of becoming my vizir, a trusted advisor to my court. As you have already noted, I am a young man so I need good advice."

For a moment nobody spoke. When Ali found his voice, it was a whisper. "I don't understand. Please get up, Your Majesty."

The Sultan got to his feet. "As a Dream Weaver, Ali, the royal blood of Luman flows in your veins."

Ali's mouth fell open. "Royal blood?"

"Luman came to me last night in a dream. Your father. He showed me all that has happened to you and he asked me to meet you here in this garden."

Ali sucked in a quick breath. "My father? Did he have a message for me?"

The Sultan smiled and indicated the flowers. "Will you gather those for me?" he asked.

Ali scooped an armful of the long-stemmed roses from the lawn where the Sultan had placed them.

Sultan Mehmed arranged the spray of roses in Ali's arms so that they looked rich and vibrant. "He did have a message for you. He told me that he wants you to take these roses to the Shade Garden."

Ali frowned, puzzled. "That's a strange thing to ask. What will I do with them when I get there?"

"That, he did not tell me. You will have to decide for yourself. Your friend Demetri can stay and help me here in the Rose Garden."

Sultan Mehmed gave Ali directions and sent him off along one of the paths leading away from where they stood. His feet scrunched on the gravel path and birds chirped in the tall boxwood hedges. Ali navigated his way through the maze until he came to the aptly named shade garden: a courtyard with a small, square central pond around which were four ornate divans shaded by tall conifers.

A young woman with an embroidered silk scarf over her head sat reading an illustrated manuscript on one of the couches.

She looked up at the sound of Ali's approach.

Ali's heart leaped into his throat. It was the Lady Ashye. *His* Rose.

She jumped to her feet, the manuscript falling to the ground, and gaped at him in disbelief.

Ali tried to say something but his mouth was dry and the words did not come out. His heart was pounding in his chest and his stomach was aflutter. He opened and closed his mouth but didn't know what to say. She was probably still angry with him.

He offered her the roses. "These are for you."

But she swept them aside and threw her arms around him.

32. Ali and Rose

The lavish inner palace of Sultan Mehmed, hidden behind a high stone wall fortified with several towers and ceremonial gates, was surrounded by gardens full of colourful flowers, ornate pools and tinkling fountains. It contained two *hamams*, two kitchens, separate quarters for the men, a harem for the women, and apartments for the attendant eunuchs.

Ali stood waiting nervously in the Sultan's reception room with Demetri, Omar Agha, and the palace Imam. He glanced around the chamber, uncomfortable with the extravagance. The ceiling was painted a deep blue with ground lapis lazuli, studded with stars of polished precious stones. The walls were tiled in a blue, white and turquoise mosaic pattern, sparkling with inset pieces of lapis lazuli, white marble, sapphires and gold.

The Sultan's gilt throne stood on a variegated marble dais at the head of the room, cushioned with scarlet brocade, its edges and tassels decorated with emeralds, rubies and pearls. Exquisite hand-knotted carpets were hung on the walls and strewn on the white marble floor, along with numerous brightly coloured pillows.

Ali flexed his fingers, curling and uncurling them, wishing time would speed up and he could get this pomp and ceremony over with.

Sultan Mehmed swept into the chamber, flanked by his personal Janissary guards, followed by the palace pages who attended to his every need. He was resplendent in a long crimson kaftan woven with gold and silver thread, studded with gems. On his head, he wore an oversized onion-bulb white turban.

"Let's get down to business," the Sultan said. Rather than sit on his throne, he stood with Ali and the others. He turned to Omar Agha. "You have agreed to the marriage and are satisfied with the terms of the contract?"

Omar Agha put his hand to his heart and bowed. "More than satisfied, Your Imperial Majesty. Yusuf fulfils the prophecy and he and my daughter are in love."

Every time they called him Yusuf, Ali thought they were talking about someone else and had to remind himself that was his real name.

The Sultan beamed. "Excellent. All that remains is to finalise the payment of the *mehir*."

"I have no wealth to speak of," Ali said.

"Without a *mehir*," the grey-bearded Imam said, "the marriage contract cannot be finalised." He flicked a piece of lint from his long black robe.

"Which is why," the Sultan said, "I am providing a more than acceptable dowry." He clapped his hands three times.

A quartet of gaudily dressed musicians entered the chamber and struck up a classical tune. One played a *ney* flute, another plucked a long-necked *tanbur* lute, the third fiddled a *rebab* with a bow, and a *davul* drummer beat time. The music was joyful and merry, celebrating the occasion.

Behind them, an enormous bare-chested black eunuch, glistening with fragrant oils, escorted the Lady Ashye and her mother, the Begüm Fatima, into the chamber, followed by a retinue of ladies-in-waiting. Ashye, or Rose as Ali still thought of her, was dressed in layers of sheer silk with a thin *yaşmak* veil covering her face and head.

"It is agreed," Omar Agha said.

Ali's face lit up with a wide grin and he felt a lightness in his chest.

Beneath her transparent veil, the Lady Ashye's green eyes sparkled and gleamed. She gave a small deferential bow. "How soon can we be married, Father?"

"I'm afraid you'll have to patient," Sultan Mehmed said.

"I am leaving with my army in two days to do battle with my brother Suleyman. Your father and his Janissaries are joining me, of course, and as my new vizir, Yusuf is coming with us too."

Lady Ashye's shoulders slumped.

"My number one priority is to restore the empire and bring peace to Anatolia," the Sultan said without apology. "Suleyman holds both Bursa and Ankara, where his power and strength grow day by day as he prepares to try to wrest control from me."

Ali's mind reeled. He felt anxious about the role he had been thrust into, about his dreaming abilities. He still felt guilty about Hasan the fisherman's death. He had done what his mother's spirit had asked, followed Luman's guidance, and unfettered his dreams to defeat Savich, save Rose from a terrible fate, and release his father to become the new Luman. But his dreaming ability still felt wild and uncontrollable.

He swallowed. It scared him. The responsibility weighed heavily.

Three gemeyes swooped into the chamber, chirping and singing. Their metallic plumes glinted and sparkled as they caught the light, their emerald eyes ablaze. Their arrival lightened Ali's mood, helped him recapture the joy of the moment.

After everything that had happened, he and Rose were to be wed. They would be husband and wife, lovers. He glanced at her with a silly grin, his legs suddenly weak.

She smiled coyly back at him, a yearning expression in her eyes.

One of the gemeyes settled on his shoulder, another on Rose's, and the third on Demetri's. They cooed and preened, emitting palpable feelings of joy and happiness.

"You are both chosen," Sultan Mehmed said, beaming. "This is an auspicious day."

Rose's father and mother, the Agha and the Begüm, swapped happy glances, unable to hide their pride.

"What about Demetri?" Ali asked. "It looks like he is chosen as well."

The Sultan appraised the one-eyed boy. "That's up to you," he said to Ali. "You are vizir now, Yusuf. You can make him anything you like. Demetri could be your valet, your page, even your counsellor."

Ali grinned at Demetri. "Well, my friend, how would you like a job?"

Demetri punched him playfully on the arm. "I thought I already was your counsellor. Where would you be now without my advice?"

"Done," the Sultan said. He turned to Ali. "Is there anything else I can do for you before we end these proceedings?"

"Please, Your Majesty, I prefer to be called Ali rather than Yusuf," he said.

"And I prefer to be called Rose," the Lady Ashye said, lowering her almond-shaped eyes in deference.

Sultan Mehmed frowned. "Your birth names are on record, they are the names the court officials and palace servants will know you by. However, I'm sure you will know each other as Ali and Rose. And perhaps your close friends will know you by those pet names too."

Ali looked at Rose and grinned. She beamed back at him, her cheeks aglow.

Epilogue

The fierce Anatolian sun shone down from a cloudless cerulean sky, bleaching colour from the rugged, arid plateau of Cappadocia, north of the Taurus Mountains. The horizon shimmered in the heat. It was an otherworldly landscape, pocked with weirdly shaped rock towers, caves and valleys. Like no other place on earth.

Jagged hoodoos, known by some as fairy chimneys, protruded from the baked volcanic landscape. Sculpted by millions of years of erosion, some were like massive fossilised dragon's teeth, others towering stems with mushroom-like tops, while several were conical monoliths. All were alien in appearance.

Many were honeycombed with caves, tunnels and grottos, their volcanic tuff stone carved out by troglodyte inhabitants. But now, during this time of war and unrest, the hoodoos were mostly abandoned, the people who recently inhabited these towers choosing to live in the relative safety of the vast catacombs tunnelled deep beneath the surface of Cappadocia.

A bored goatherd, a boy of eleven or twelve, squatted in the mouth of a cave in a valley, its shade protecting him from the heat of the sun. He scratched random patterns on the bleached ground with a stick. A dozen or so shaggy, long-eared goats foraged nearby, spreading out to nibble at the sparse grassy steppe plants, wild thyme and sage, stringy juniper and wild almond shrubs.

Something caught the boy's eye and he looked up. A single, lone cloud scudded across the sky.

But wait…

Was it a cloud? It looked more like a swirl of charcoal-coloured smoke, writhing and twisting in the still air. It began to circle the Cappadocian plateau, gradually descending lower and lower until it hovered over a twisted, pinkish stone tower pocked with holes like lotus root.

The goatherd rose to his feet and stepped out of the cave for a better look.

The whirlwind of smoke darted into an opening near the top of the warped conical monolith. A moment later, a dazzling red light, like the furnace-hot heart of an active volcano, shone out from every opening in the tower, glowing with such eerie intensity it cast ruddy beams of fire onto the surrounding desert landscape.

The boy shivered, frozen to the spot, a chill running down his spine.

There came a loud *whoosh*, and the fiery light coalesced, crackling into a single ruby brilliance, as bright as erupting lava. It snaked its way down through the hoodoo, an eerie red glow emanating from the windows and fissures in the twisted monolith, until gradually it faded, like the embers of a fire.

The goats began to bleat. The shepherd boy snapped out of his trance and hurriedly rounded up his flock. He uttered a brief prayer and herded them across the valley, away from this inexplicable incident, back towards the shelter of their underground home. He was not sure what he had witnessed, but he did not want to hang around to find out. When he took the goats out tomorrow, he decided, he would take them in the opposite direction, away from this place.

Glossary

Afyonkarahisar – A city in central Turkey whose name literally translates as "Opium Black Fortress". Afyonkarahisar has grown opium poppies for centuries and is still the world's largest producer of pharmaceutical opium.

Akçe – A silver coin which was the main monetary unit of the Ottoman Empire.

Agha – A title of honour for a high-ranking civilian or military officer in the Ottoman Empire.

Akyatan Gölü – Akyatan Lagoon is a 14700-hectare wetland area located at the south-eastern coast of Mediterranean Turkey near the city of Adana.

Alinazik – A spicy traditional Turkish dish of smoked eggplant and lamb stew.

Amanus Mountains – Medieval name for the Nur Mountains in south-eastern Turkey.

Amasya – A city in northern Turkey in a narrow valley on the bank of the Yeşilırmak River. In the early Ottoman period a Sultan's sons were sent here to govern and gain experience. Sultan Mehmed ruled in Amasya during the 11-year Ottoman civil war between him and his brothers.

Anatolia – The ancient name for what is now the Asian part of the Republic of Türkiye.

Araba – A covered wagon or cart drawn by horses or oxen.

Aşure – A sweet Turkish porridge or dessert, also known as *Ashure* or Noah's Pudding, made from grains, dried fruit and nuts.

Ayasofya – Located in Istanbul (Constantinople) and known in English as the Hagia Sophia, it was built in 537 as a Christian cathedral and later converted to a mosque complete with towering minarets by the Ottomans.

Baksheesh – A small sum of money given or as alms to the poor or as a tip.

Bādiyah Ash-Shām – The Arabic name for the vast Syrian Desert.

Baglama – A Turkish stringed musical instrument similar to an English lute or a Greek *bouzouki*.

Balık Buğulama – A traditional Turkish fish stew cooked with onion, garlic and vegetables.

Bedouin – A group of nomadic Arab tribespeople who have traditionally inhabited the deserts of North Africa and the Middle East.

Begüm – An aristocratic title which applies to the wife or daughter of a Beg or Bey, a Turkish tribal chief.

Beshbarmak – A traditional Central Asian nomad dish of boiled noodles and meat, usually horse or mutton, spiced with onion sauce.

Bey – Chieftain or leader of a province or ethnic group.

Beyler Palace – The palace of the Ottoman princes, located on the right bank of the Yeşilırmak River in Amasya.

Boza – A thick fermented grain drink with a low alcohol content and slightly acidic sweet taste, popular in Eastern Europe and Central Asia.

Byzantine stavraton – High-denomination silver coin from Constantinople (formerly Byzantium), the capital city of the Byzantine (Eastern Roman) Empire.

Caravanserai – A roadside or city inn where travellers and traders in Asia and Southeast Europe could stay overnight in safety when travelling.

Çelebi – An Ottoman Turkish title that means gentleman, often given to the sons of the sultan and other notable men.

Chagatai – See **Jagatai.**

Davul – A large double-sided drum used in the traditional folk music of Turkey, Iran and Eastern Europe.

Dervish – A member of a Sufi Muslim order who has taken vows of poverty and austerity, famous for their ecstatic ceremonies that include trances, dancing, whirling and howling.

Divan – A Turkish or Middle Eastern couch made of a mattress to sit on with cushions to lean against.

Ducat – A gold coin used widely in trade across Europe and parts of the Middle East during the Middle Ages.

Dzhabe – A breed of Kazakh horse, also called a Jabe, known for its endurance and strength, as well as its high milk and meat yield.

Efendi – A title of respect for a high-ranking or learned person, roughly equivalent to 'sir' in English.

Edirne – A city on the north-western border of present-day Turkey, it served as the capital city of the Ottoman Empire from 1363 to 1453.

Ezan – Turkish name for the Islamic call to prayer, the *adhan*, recited by a müezzin at prescribed times of the day.

Fakir – A Sufi Muslim ascetic who renounces worldly possessions.

Gâvur – A term used in the Ottoman Empire as a slur against non-Muslims.

Golden Horde – The European name for the Mongol Empire established by Genghis Khan and expanded by his heirs.

Gozleme – A traditional Turkish savory flatbread snack filled with a thin layer of meat, vegetables or spices and fried on a hot griddle.

Hamam – A communal sauna/bathing area commonly known as a Turkish Bath. Traditional *hamams* typically contain a relaxation room heated by hot air, an even hotter sauna-like room, and hot and cold bathing pools.

Harem – Household rooms for women in a Muslim home. The only adult males allowed access are close relations and eunuch attendants.

Horned-Hand – A hand gesture known as the "Sign of the Horns" made by holding the middle and ring fingers down with the thumb and extending the index and little fingers. It is used traditionally to ward off bad luck and the "evil eye".

Imam – A Muslim religious leader.

İskenderūn – A Turkish city on the Mediterranean coast in the Gulf of İskenderūn, at the foot of the Nur Mountains (Amanus Mountains). Historically it was also known as Alexandretta and Scanderoon.

Jagatai – A person from the Mongol/Turkic Chagatai Khanate, or kingdom, that ruled part of Central Asia in the late Middle Ages.

Janissary – An elite Turkish infantryman serving as an Ottoman Sultan's bodyguard or household guard between the 14th and 19th centuries. Janissary troops also became a key part of the Ottoman army.

Jinn – A Genie or Djinn is a spirit or demon of Arabian folklore, often depicted in fairy tales as trapped in a lamp or bottle.

Kalpak – A tall cap of felt or sheepskin traditionally worn by the men of various Turkish and Central Asian ethnic groups.

Kazakhs – A Turkic ethnic group of people from the northern parts of Central Asia (Kazakhstan, Uzbekistan, Mongolia and parts of Russia).

Kilij – A Middle Eastern single-edged, curved-blade sabre or slashing sword, similar to a *scimitar*.

Korykos – Also spelled Corycus, was an ancient Mediterranean port city in Anatolia. The town of Kızkalesi in Mersin Province, Turkey, is now located on the site.

Kumis – A fermented dairy drink traditionally made from mare's milk by Turkic and Mongol people.

Lamellar – A type of armour made from small plates of iron or leather laced together.

Lapis Lazuli – A deep-blue semi-precious gemstone.

Maghreb – Northwest African region that includes Algeria, Libya, Morocco and Tunisia.

Mamluk Sultanate – A medieval empire started by slave soldiers who rose up and seized power from their Muslim rulers and ruled much of Egypt, Lebanon, Jordan, Israel, Palestine, and parts of Turkey (1250–1517).

Manakish – Flat bread topped with ground meat or cheese sprinkled with thyme, which some people call Middle Eastern pizza.

Mercimek Çorbasi – Turkish red lentil soup traditionally made with onions, potato and carrot.

Mehir – A mandatory payment in Islamic weddings from the groom (or his family) to the bride. Similar to a dowry or "bride price" in other cultures. It can be paid in money, possessions or both.

Müezzin – The person at a mosque who leads and recites the call to prayer for Muslims.

Nazar – An eye-shaped bead or amulet believed to protect against the evil eye. It is common in Turkey, Eastern Europe and the Middle East.

Ney – An ancient Middle Eastern end-blown flute.

Osmanli – The original Turkish name for the Ottoman Empire, named after Sultan Osman I, the founder of the Ottoman dynasty.

Pasha – A title designating high-ranking Ottomans such as governors, generals and dignitaries.

Pilav – A rice dish cooked in broth, usually with vegetables and spices.

Rebab – A Central Asian fiddle with up to three strings and played with a bow.

Romani – The Romani are an ethnic group of nomadic people originally from northern India, but now spread widely throughout the world. They are commonly known as Gypsies, a term many find offensive.

Sea of Murmans – The old name for the Barents Sea, located off the northern coast of Norway and Russia.

Şalvar – Traditional Turkish baggy trousers, usually gathered at the ankles.

Scimitar A curved-blade sabre used in Middle East countries.

Simit – A circular bagel-shaped bread coated with sesame, poppy or sunflower seeds.

Tabar – Ottoman and Persian long-handled battle axe with large single- or double-sided crescent-shaped blades.

Tajiki – A version of the Persian language spoken in Tajikistan and Uzbekistan by Tajiks, an Iranian ethnic group native to those Central Asian regions.

Tanbur – A long-necked string instrument similar to a lute.

Tarator – A yogurt sauce, dip or soup usually made with cucumber, ground nuts, garlic, dill and other herbs.

Tavla – The Turkish name for backgammon (and its variations), possibly the oldest board game in the world.

Tengri – Primary deity, along with Umay (the Earth Mother), of the early Turkic shamanistic religion known as Tengrism. Tengri (also known as Kök-Tangri) was the Sky God, the creator and Heavenly-Father.

Timur Lenk – Also known as Tamerlane or Timur the Lame, was a Turco-Mongol military leader from Central Asia. He was a brutal warlord who conquered most of the Muslim world, including Persia, Turkey and parts of India. In doing so, it is estimated that his army killed 17 million people.

Turkoman horse – A breed of horse from the steppes of Central Asia, noted for its toughness and endurance.

Uzbeg – Also spelled Uzbek, is a Turkic ethnic group from Central Asia. Today they make up the primary population of Uzbekistan. After the death of Timur Lenk and the break-up of his Timurid Empire, they conquered much of Central Asia.

Vizir (Visier) – A counsellor or high-ranking political adviser in Ottoman Turkey.

Yaşmak – A thin two-piece Turkish veil, one part tied across the forehead and draped over the head and the other tied across the face under the nose.

Author's Notes

Although *Dream Weaver* is a fantasy story, many of its elements are real. It takes place in 1405 in Anatolia—the medieval name for what is now the Republic of Türkiye—at a time of great political and social instability. Here are some things about the book that are true, and some that are not:

Characters

Ali, his mother and father (in his various guises), Demetri, Rose/Lady Ashye, Luman, Omar Agha, Fedar, Khasis, and Savich are all fictional characters.

The Ottoman Sultan Bayezid I and his sons Mehmed, Suleyman, Musa, Isa and Mustafa were all real people, but my portrayal of Mehmed is largely fictional.

The nomadic Turko-Mongol conqueror Timur Lenk was also a real person. He waged brutal military campaigns across Central Asia, much of the Middle East, and parts of South Asia and Eastern Europe. He might have taken over the known world had he lived long enough, but he died in early 1405 on his way to invade China.

The Ottomans

The Ottoman Empire was founded in 1299 by Sultan Osman Ghazi, ruler of a small Turkoman principality in north western Anatolia. From that early beginning the empire grew through military conquest to become one of the largest, richest, and most powerful the world has ever seen. It lasted for over 600 years, and, at its peak, the Ottomans ruled much of West Asia, Southeast Europe, the Middle East and North Africa. But the empire almost collapsed in 1402 when Bayezid was defeated by Timur and died as his prisoner a short time later.

The Ottoman leadership vacuum created by these events resulted in a civil war among Bayezid's sons (known as the Ottoman Interregnum) which lasted almost 11 years. Mehmed finally killed or defeated his brothers and crowned himself Sultan Mehmed I in 1413.

Janissaries

The Janissaries were an elite Ottoman military corps. They were initially formed in the late 14th century to be the Sultan's imperial bodyguards. Unlike most soldiers of the period, they wore colourful uniforms with unique tall white felt hats that folded back and hung down their backs. Although the Janissaries were an infantry rather than cavalry corps, many of them were also skilled horsemen. Over time the Janissaries became a key part of the Ottoman army and were recognised and feared as the best-trained soldiers in Europe.

Slaves

Slavery, repugnant as it is today, was an institution in the Ottoman Empire for most of its existence. Indeed, the growth of their economy was largely based on exploiting slaves as soldiers, farm hands, tradespeople, domestic servants, public servants, and sex and galley slaves. Even the elite Janissary corps was made up of children forcibly recruited from the families of Ottoman Christian subjects, who were made to convert to Islam and rigorously trained to grow up as soldiers. Hundreds of thousands of men, women and children entered Ottoman slavery as the booty of war. North African people were stolen in raids across the Mediterranean Sea, and European slaves were purchased from Barbary pirates who attacked and kidnapped people from European coastal towns.

Religion

The Ottoman Empire was a caliphate (an Islamic state ruled by a single religious and political leader), with other religious and ethnic communities operating under its governance. At times Muslims, Christians, Jews and other religions lived in relative harmony, but at other times the Ottomans practised active religious and ethnic persecution.

Many Turkish and Mongol ethnic groups were adherents of Tengrism, a religion based on the worship of a sky god called Tengri who they considered to be the creator of the world and the personification of the universe. Followers believed in a reverence for nature and a desire to live in harmony with the world.

Landscape and Places

All the cities and towns and most of the locations in this book are real places, and I am lucky to have travelled across Turkey and visited some of them. I must admit, however, that a few scenes, including the tunnels beneath the Korykos fortress, the Bird Boulders, the Lost River, the dungeon beneath Afyonkarahisar, and Luman's home and the gemeye chamber beneath the desert are products of my imagination.

Korykos

Ali's home town of Korykos was an ancient Mediterranean port city in Anatolia. It is now called Kızkalesi, named after the ancient Maiden's Castle on the small island off the coast. The ruins of Korykos Castle, the imposing mainland fortress that once protected the city, still rise above the golden sands of the beach, although no one has reported finding any tunnels beneath it.

Akyatan Gölü

The Akyatan Lagoon wetlands area is now a 14,700-hectare protected wildlife refuge, which provides breeding grounds for large numbers of fish, turtles, frogs, birds, and many other animal species.

İskenderūn

İskenderūn (formerly Alexandretta), the town where Ali meets Demetri, still exists today. It was originally founded by Alexander the Great after he defeated the Persian Darius III in 333 BC and served as a major shipping port to the west for overland trade from Iran and India until modern transport routes superseded it.

Bādiyah Ash-Shām

Bādiyah Ash-Shām is the Arabic name for the vast inhospitable Syrian Desert (also known as the North Arabian Desert), an arid wasteland which stretches some 500,000 square kilometres across parts of Syria, Jordan, Saudi Arabia and Iraq. The nomadic Arab Bedouin people are believed to have originated there and some tribes still remain in the region.

Afyonkarahisar

This city in central Turkey is named after the fortress that stands 200 metres high on top of a craggy hill of dark volcanic rock. Its name literally translates as "Opium Black Fortress" or perhaps "Black Castle of Opium", because the fortress overlooks a landscape that has grown opium poppies for centuries. The castle was valued for its defensive fortification and was the site of many battles over the centuries. It was conquered by Sultan Bayezid I in 1392, but was lost to the Ottomans after Timur Lenk's invasion in 1402. Because of its name, location, and availability it seemed to me to be the perfect base for Savich and his henchmen.

Amasya

The Beyler Palace in Amasya was Mehmed's stronghold during the Ottoman Interregnum. It was surrounded by a high wall enclosing imperial gardens that were said to contain pools and fountains and a wealth of roses. There is no record of a maze in the gardens, but accounts of that period are scarce, so it's always possible there might have been one. By 1825 the once opulent palace had been destroyed by earthquakes and was little more than ruins and rubble.

Food and Produce

Turkish cuisine—a delicious fusion of ingredients, flavours and techniques from Central Asia, the Mediterranean, the Balkans, and the Middle East—is largely derived from Ottoman cooking, and the recipes for many traditional dishes are hundreds of years old. All of the produce, food and drinks in this book are authentic and I am lucky to have seen and eaten some of them when I travelled through Turkey. My biggest regret is that I could not include Turkish delight in the story because it was not invented until the late 18th century.

Plants and Animals

Most of the plants and animals (including the sand vipers!) in *Dream Weaver* are indigenous to the locations and habitats I have used. And, yes, tiger sharks have been found in the Mediterranean Sea, but they are very rare. Tiger sharks are considered to be man-eaters, second only to the great white shark in the number of attacks on people, and recent scientific research has found they aren't always loners and sometimes do hunt in packs. As for the sluglows and gemeyes, sadly, they are not real.

Or are they…?

Acknowledgements

This novel has had a long gestation and it would not have been half the book it is without the help and support of many people. It began as a short story decades ago, but was put aside because Ali's story was incomplete. In the intervening years his story grew slowly in my mind, bit by bit, until his tale finally emerged. I owe thanks and gratitude to the following people for their generous advice and feedback on earlier versions or sections of the manuscript that helped bring *Dream Weaver* to life: Justin Ackroyd, Belinda Bolliger, Jack Dann, Garry Disher, Rebecca Fraser, Sarah Lane, Sean McMullen, Deborah Sheldon, Lucy Sussex, and Janeen Webb. Thanks are also owed to Eugen Bacon, Isobelle Carmody, Sue Drakeford, Jason Franks, Richard Harland, George Ivanoff, Kirstyn McDermott, Jason Nahrung, the late Anne Paulsen, Aaron Sterns, Anna Tambour, Shaun Tan, Kaaron Warren, Sean Williams and Maurice Xanthos for their support and inspiration. Thanks also to the passionate IFWG Publishing team including publisher Gerry Huntman, copy editor extraordinaire Noel Osualdini, Stephen McCracken, and cover designer and illustrator Steve Santiago. And last, but not least, thank you to everyone who has made the time to read this book. I hope you enjoyed reading it as much as I enjoyed writing it.

Steven Paulsen is an award-winning speculative fiction writer. His bestselling spooky children's book, *The Stray Cat* (Lothian/ Hachette), illustrated by Hugo and Oscar Award winning artist Shaun Tan, has seen publication in several English and foreign language editions. His horror, science fiction and dark fantasy short stories, which Jack Dann describes as rocket-fuelled with narrative drive, have appeared in books and magazines around the world. The best of his weird tales can be found in his short story collection, *Shadows on the Wall* (IFWG Publishing Australia, 2018), which won the Australian Horror Writers Association Shadows Award for Best Collected Work. Readers can find out more about Steven's work at: www.stevenpaulsen.com.